Marlet Ashley, B.A., B.Ed., M.A., earned an undergraduate degree in psychology at the University of Windsor and taught at St. Clair College of Applied Arts and Technology. Marlet earned an M.A. in English Literature and Creative Writing at the University of Windsor, and taught creative writing there as a sessional instructor. After moving to Vancouver, B.C., she became a tenured instructor of literature and composition at Kwantlen Polytechnic University in Surrey, B.C. Her first novel is *The Right Kind of Crazy* (2018). Her children's book series includes *Revelry on the Estuary—The Interlopers, Trumpeters' Tribulations, Penelope Piper's Great Adventure, Henri Sings the Blues,* and *A Pirate's Life for Gabby*—as well as a children's Christmas book—*Must Be Christmas*—and *Robin and Ruthie Ride the Bus.* Marlet is the author of the Canadian edition of *Literature and the Writing Process,* published by Pearson Prentice Hall in Toronto. Additionally, she is a member of the Federation of BC Writers.

Marlet has been a guest lecturer at Elder College at North Island College. She also conducted workshops for the Comox Valley Writers Society's conference at North Island College in 2018, 2019 and 2020. As one of the three finalists for the 2012 John Kenneth Galbraith Literary Award, she was also the recipient of an honorable mention in the Lorian Hemmingway Short Story Competition in 2018 and the *Writers' Digest* Literary Short Fiction Contest in 2020. A contributing member of The Group of Glacier Writers, she has three titles in *Re-Collections*, a collection of short stories (2021). Her story *'Design'* in the RCLAS 2022 Write-On short fiction competition won first place, and she was the fiction judge for the 2023 competition.

Marlet lives in Comox, BC., with her husband, artist Pieter Molenaar.

For my children and my children's children.

Marlet Ashley

The Liberation of Oliver Rook

Austin Macauley Publishers

LONDON * CAMBRIDGE * NEW YORK * SHARJAH

Copyright © Marlet Ashley 2024

All rights reserved. No part of this publication may be reproduced, distributed, or transmitted in any form or by any means, including photocopying, recording, or other electronic or mechanical methods, without the prior written permission of the publisher, except in the case of brief quotations embodied in critical reviews and certain other non-commercial uses permitted by copyright law. For permission requests, write to the publisher.

Any person who commits any unauthorized act in relation to this publication may be liable to criminal prosecution and civil claims for damages.

This is a work of fiction. Names, characters, businesses, places, events, locales, and incidents are either the products of the author's imagination or used in a fictitious manner. Any resemblance to actual persons, living or dead, or actual events is purely coincidental.

Ordering Information
Quantity sales: Special discounts are available on quantity purchases by corporations, associations, and others. For details, contact the publisher at the address below.

Publisher's Cataloging-in-Publication data
Ashley, Marlet
The Liberation of Oliver Rook

ISBN 9798886938623 (Paperback)
ISBN 9798886938630 (ePub e-book)

Library of Congress Control Number: 2023916857

www.austinmacauley.com/us

First Published 2024
Austin Macauley Publishers LLC
40 Wall Street, 33rd Floor, Suite 3302
New York, NY 10005
USA

mail-usa@austinmacauley.com
+1 (646) 5125767

As with all of us, so much of what I know about human nature comes from experience. However, I have my many psychology instructors to thank along with my numerous students of psychology who suffered under my early attempts at teaching. While much of this book focuses on the fallout from mental illness, it was never my intention to blame the victim. If this book points out the weaknesses in our present mental health care, child protection, and law-enforcement systems, systems that allow the innocent to be subjected horrendously to the effects of mental illness, and a push for change results, then it has served a purpose.

Thanks go to the Comox Valley Writers Society and to the fiction writing group: Beverley, Cathy, Kathy, Ken, Kunio, John, and others who have come into and gone from the group. Your feedback has been invaluable. Thanks also to Ruth Anne and Beverley and other beta readers whose help I greatly appreciate.

Many thanks to my husband and my sons for their patience, love, and support.

Chapter 1

Nothing was unusual about a man hoisting a backpack and pulling a suitcase toward Vancouver's Waterfront Skytrain Station in the late afternoon. Not a soul would have stopped him to ask where he was going or what he was leaving behind. Why would they? He appeared much like many others walking with purpose, a destination in mind. But on this crisp fall day, he did not feel the unassuming way he looked. Rather, he felt conspicuous in his attempt to avoid drawing attention to himself. He also felt as a child might on the verge of an adventure, yet he was too guarded to allow this scrap of excitement to show in case his plans and what might come after fell through. He kept a straight face, a poker face, one that did not reveal the conflicting emotions that besieged him.

He looked up as he drew near his preliminary destination. Between the buildings, the sky appeared that particular shade of blue, dense and heavy with the anticipation of approaching finality, apparent only in the autumn as the light tilts toward the end of day. Clouds hung harmlessly, yet, always on the lookout, he searched them for signs of ominous weather as he waited for the traffic light to change.

Oliver was not unpleasant looking. A few of his former colleagues told him he looked like a younger and much stockier version of Dick Van Dyke because of his long face and dark hair and because he often had a smile and a joke to tell, the way with most comedians, laughing and joking to disguise some deep hurt or profound injury life had inflicted upon them. He was no exception. In his case, his colleagues knew a little about his situation and had been witness to some of the struggles he'd endured. They had not been without compassion, ignoring as best they could the ever-deepening web of exhaustion lining his face.

His clothes said little about him except that he had dressed well for autumn and not necessarily for comfort—an olive green and rust tweed jacket with brown suede patches on the elbows. It was an old style but neat. A little too constricting, his necktie added a touch of formality although he'd rarely worn one when lecturing. His pale-yellow shirt was a little too tight at his neck and across his chest, but it was the only one he had left after packing. It went along well with his dark corduroy pants, soft leather shoes, and chocolate-colored flat cap. He was not fashionable, but, he decided, he did not appear eccentric. He measured his gait making it steady and unhurried even if the urge to bolt like a racehorse leaving its counterparts behind was strong. He strove to look as if he were not running away.

Oliver rehearsed the route he had taken so as to remember it when the inevitable questions were asked—the bus from his home on the university campus had brought him to the transfer point at Broadway and Granville. His streetcar had then hummed its way to downtown Vancouver, its doors hissing open at every stop along the way then screeching closed, metal on metal. From the stop at Granville and Georgia, he'd walked the several blocks to Waterfront Station to catch the Skytrain.

It would have been much easier and faster to take a cab from home to the Via Rail station, but the city he had once loved drew him like a magnet. The busyness of downtown infused him with excitement and dread. He felt himself a stranger in the place where he had been born and bred. Vancouver had changed so much over the years. Newly-constructed towering buildings obscured the view across Burrard Inlet to the mountains beyond, making him feel doubly confined. As a child, he would look across to the blue and sometimes snow-covered mountains and wonder what was beyond. He and his younger brother Derek planned their expedition, gathered what they thought was mountain-climbing equipment, and plotted to begin by conquering The Lions. Derek claimed the West Lion, and Oliver settled for the East Lion, the lower of the two peaks.

But it was when they were old enough to go skiing on their first public school trip that they'd found out what they were up against. Mountains upon mountains all the way to Whistler. At the top of Blackcomb, their chaperone, thrilled to expose them to the miles upon miles of snow-covered peaks, could hardly be expected to understand the boys' profound dismay. The young mountaineers would not have made it very far. After that trip, they never spoke of their mountain-climbing plans again. Such was the overwhelming power of the massive ridges, peaks, and craigs. Derek turned to the ocean for his escape, his livelihood. Oliver remained behind, cowered by downtown glass and steel edifices as well as the earth's violent upheavals north of the city.

Gastown remained the same, however, with its brick and tiny cubby-hole souvenir shops. He'd often wondered how they managed to exist selling cheap plastic knickknacks and oddities. Speculation had it that many were fronts for more sinister activities. Yet he loved the confusion of milling tourists and workers rushing to their jobs. The sound of the steam clock whistling the hours, half hours, and quarter hours. Good memories here. The children had loved visiting a curiosity shop in the old cobblestoned section. Down in the basement, a wall of drawers kept the three of them busy for an afternoon. He'd pick up Gwendolyn so she could reach the top drawers, and she'd take out small treasures to show her brother. Then he'd lift Gavin to do the same. Miniature cars, Jacob's ladders, whistles, rings, mouth organs, kazoos, and puzzles—a different surprise in each drawer. Several times a year Oliver brought them to this magical place where they chose one trinket each after looking in every one of a hundred drawers. They did not mind the cramped and cluttered room. But as the kids got older, they came less often, then not at all. He missed those days.

Even the Bay's snooty coffee baristas selling pods for high-end coffee makers made him smile. They had flair enough to intimidate even the most pompous professional. It was all pretense, all marketing, all part of the city circus. If he could shed the awful memories of the last three decades, perhaps he could love Vancouver again, but too much was associated with it and the familiar streets, with the ocean and with the mountains that stood guard to the north.

If someone were to stop him and ask his reason for traveling, he would not be shy about giving a short version. He would tell them he was, like an amphibian shedding its too-small skin, leaving his old life behind and setting off to lead his new one, the life he had been meant to live all along but from which he had become sidetracked. What he would not tell them was that he had warned her, telling her that when the kids were gone and all debts were paid, he would leave. What she did after that was her business. With these words, he'd tried to absolve himself. This was what Oliver Eastmund, at the age of sixty-six, thought as he caught a glimpse of himself in the tall windows of the building that housed the Waterfront Station.

The late-afternoon crowds slowed him down a bit, but he was early and not hurrying. He did not push his way through but allowed the masses to move him along to the platform he needed. Everyone was going home after a long hard day, and so was Oliver although it would take him much longer to get there.

The Skytrain left Waterfront Station, sped toward Terminal, and there Oliver crossed to the Pacific Railway Station. He took a deep breath and paused before entering the crowded building, then made his way through the echoing main corridor, carefully dodging porters rushing with carts and excusing himself as he passed doddering pedestrians. He paused to hold a door open for an elderly couple burdened with luggage. Smiling, he pointed for them the way to the bus wickets also at the station. The frail couple reminded him of his parents, the age they would have been had they lived beyond his own age. His father had died from septic shock when, while gardening, he'd cut himself, just a small innocent-looking cut. It had become infected and his whole body filled with the bacteria. Septicemia. Only a few short months after he'd retired at sixty, his ashes were scattered in Stanley Park near Lost Lagoon, his favorite place to walk.

One year later, Oliver's mother died from pneumonia after contracting the flu. It seemed life had had little purpose for her after her husband was gone. Oliver and his brother Derek were left, adults making their own way through life. Oliver chose a life of stability, loyalty, steadfastness, and intellectual pursuits while Derek danced his way through life, flirting with excitement and danger along the way. Derek was the adventurer, always on the move. A risk-taker who, after years of extreme sports, finally settled down enough to become an entrepreneur, designing, developing and selling surf and snowboards and other outdoor equipment for the next generation. Theirs had been a happy childhood, better than average, better than the childhood of Oliver's own children.

His father and mother had worked hard and been cautious with spending. His parents had contributed a great deal to both his and Derek's university educations, certainly more than he could say he'd done for his kids. From Oliver's perspective at this stage of his life, his childhood had been idyllic. His mother stayed home until he and his brother were in high school, then she went back to teaching kindergarten, a job she loved. She was a grounded person, loving but disciplined. Both of Oliver's parents were good role models. What, he wondered, had happened to him that he'd allowed himself to be trapped in such a hate-filled life, had made such a mess of things?

At the Via Rail booths, the line was short, so he hardly had to wait to pick up his one-way ticket to Toronto. He looked around for a restaurant or a coffee shop where he could pass the hour and twenty minutes before boarding his train, a train that would take three days to reach his destination.

In the past few decades, at every place he'd stopped for a meal or a coffee, he sat facing the door with his back to a wall. It was a defensive pose but one he chose automatically and with which he felt most comfortable. From such a seat, he could see who came in, and no one could come up behind him. He tried never to sit in a booth from which he could not escape should the need arise. At this point, he had the option of sitting wherever he liked, but old habits die hard, as the expression goes, and anywhere but his preferred place left him ill at ease.

A young server came to his table and took his order of soup and coffee. She was impatient with him when he asked her to repeat herself.

In a statement of irritation, not a question, she rolled her eyes and said, "Bread. Do you want bread with your soup?" He noticed more and more how quickly everything around him moved while he seemed stuck, unable to keep up. It had become that way at the university as well. He'd gone back to teaching face-to-face classes after the kids left home, but he found that students pushed past him and even ran into him from time to time. He avoided the stairs for fear of being knocked down. A colleague told him to wear a black suit.

"The seas part for a black suit," he'd said.

But Oliver didn't own a black suit and wasn't about to buy one for the few semesters he'd had left, so he frequently took the elevator in Chandler Hall, the building that housed most of the humanities classes. The word STAFF in gold calligraphy was painted on the old wooden doors. One day, he and Fred Findlay, a dour, antiquated professor of classical studies, got into the antediluvian contraption, and a student on crutches hobbled in after them.

Lifting one of her crutches, she said, "This is as close to a staff as I could find."

Oliver gave a chuckle then laughed aloud with her after Fred harrumphed his way out of the elevator onto the second floor. Oliver was a man who had to find joy where he could.

He finished his soup, and in spite of the server's attitude, he left a generous tip. Perhaps it would brighten her day and her outlook. Then again, after he left for the train, he thought perhaps he had just rewarded bad behavior. He was a champion at second-guessing himself. Finally, he decided, it was never wrong to be generous either with tips or kindness. He reminded himself to get into the habit of being both generous and kind as much as he could, now that he could, and he carried on. The line of half-a-dozen passengers moved onto the train, Oliver's home for the next three days. The porter looked at his ticket and pointed him toward a seat at the far end nearest what turned out to be the hospitality coach. At the opposite end was the dining car where a light dinner would be served later this evening, or so the few people boarding through his section of the car were told by the steward, a dignified yet approachable-looking man.

After an initial wave of claustrophobia, Oliver looked around the car. Double seats faced each other in pairs on either side of the aisle. Private cabins, washrooms and shower rooms made up the rest. The seats were gray, and the walls were covered in vinyl bearing a hardly-noticeable pattern of white and beige, colors likely intended to promote tranquility and to calm nervous travelers. Oliver was nervous but not about traveling. He was eager to get away, far away. No one else claimed a seat in his section, so he was alone at least until the next stop.

Settled, and as comfortable as he could be in the seat the porter would make into a berth at night, Oliver looked forward to seeing his son, Gavin, who was a lawyer and lived with his wife Theresa in Rosedale, a place redolent of privilege and wealth. Oliver's daughter, Gwendolyn, was a Ph.D. candidate in psychology at York University. He smiled slightly at the thought of seeing them soon. He was so proud of both. They'd worked hard to get where they were, but one of his many regrets was that he hadn't been able to help them out financially as much as he would have liked. Although he'd flown to Toronto several times in the four years since Gwen left home, the kids never came back to Vancouver. Who could blame them? The wonder was how long it had taken Oliver to leave.

"For God's sake, Dad, leave. Get out of there. You deserve some peace. You can come here and stay with Gavin. I'm sure he won't mind. His house is huge, and Theresa would love to see you. So would I," Gwendolyn had chided him more than once. "You could stay with me, but you'd have to share the space with me and my roommate. Student digs, you understand," she offered. Gavin and Theresa extended frequent invitations as well.

From the train, he watched East Vancouver speed by the window. Oliver thought back to how long it had taken him to get to this moment. To leave Mona took Oliver years, a lifetime, his lifetime, the children's. And hers. The kids could not get out of the house fast enough. Their grades were always excellent, top of the class both of them, most likely because they knew a scholarship was the way to freedom. They could have stayed and gone to BCU, tuition waived as it was for all children of employees and faculty. But they wanted to go far away. Oliver stayed. He stayed until he knew there was little likelihood of the children returning and needing his protection, and little chance of Mona following them to cause further havoc in their lives. He stayed until he was assured of a decent pension, retiring earlier than some of his colleagues. He stayed until the perfect moment.

To say that life with Mona had been difficult would be a laughable understatement had it not been so bad. It had been hell. When Gav and Gwen were babies, Mona's mother, Frances, familiar with Mona's condition, lived with them and cared for the babies during the day until Oliver got home and took over. Mona never worked again after the children came, neither outside the home nor inside.

Oliver fell in love completely and irrevocably with each of the children the instant he saw them. Gavin and Gwendolyn both were born with dark hair that soon fell out. They were bald for so long that Oliver worried they'd never grow hair again, but they did. Both ended up blond with eyes the same shade of blue as their mother's, but when he gazed into their eyes, as he had every day of their lives until they left home, innocence and trust shone from them. Mona had insisted on a private room for each of their births, but as soon as she was able, she'd left the hospital and left Oliver to stay in the room to care for each baby.

The first time she did this, Oliver was terrified. He had read much about the first year of a baby's life and knew in a bookish way how to care for Gavin. But to actually be left alone not only to look after an infant but to deal with his own feelings of rejection and inadequacy for not being able to foster in his wife a sense of closeness, of family, shook his view of the world, of reality. Life was not supposed to be like this, he said again and again to himself. When she left after Gwendolyn was born, Oliver was not surprised. Mona's true nature had revealed itself in the years between the children's births. Although he knew it was wrong of her to leave her newborn baby, the first inklings of relief at her absence sparked inside him as he held an infant Gwendolyn. He spoke of Mona's departure to her obstetrician, and while she agreed that it was not usual, it was not all that alarming. Mona had returned the last time, and this time would likely be no different.

Claiming post-partum depression, Mona came back in time to go home with Oliver and the new baby and avoid being reported to the Ministry of Children and Family Development by hospital staff. How he wished they or he had informed on her for abandoning her baby, but he had not been clairvoyant, just naïve. He thought he could fix their lives. If he tried harder, life would get better. It was his mantra until he finally accepted her insanity as his to live with.

Compared to later times, the years with Frances, the children's grandmother, were almost peaceful. She would often have dinner on the stove when he got home, and she sometimes helped get the children ready for bed. Bedtime, however, was Oliver's domain. He would tell them stories and ask about the best and worst parts of their day. He would crow with delight over accomplishments—"I got a star today, Daddy—" and commiserate with them over hurts and slights—"Bobby pushed me off the swing and laughed at me when I fell." When they were a little older, he would also, in as gentle and reassuring way as possible, remind them to lock their doors again if they had to get up in the night. He comforted them by saying that if ever there was an emergency, he could easily break their doors down and rescue them. While never an athlete, Oliver was solidly built and strong. How entrenched in Mona's madness they had all become. Not until looking back did it strike him that having to keep their doors locked was outrageous. At the time, it was simply a way to cope.

But Frances could not keep up with Mona or the children forever, so when Gavin and Gwendolyn were in school full days, Oliver arranged his teaching schedule around the children's school hours, and Frances left them to live out the last few years of her life in peace. Years later, online university courses became possible, and he taught from home, released from tension only when Mona went out for a day or evening. The children were never left alone with her. She could not be trusted.

He couldn't count the number of times people asked him why he simply didn't take the kids and run, and for years he debated with himself if this would have been better than staying and living in constant anxiety. It was not as if he hadn't tried. He just knew whether the three of them lived with her or not, she would be a threat. Better to keep her close and prepare for what could happen than leave, develop a false sense of wellbeing, and be ambushed. The truth was, he had tried, but the Ministry, courts, doctors, and hospitals failed. They failed him, they failed Mona, and most of all they failed the children. Justice was indeed blind. It was deaf and dumb as well. So was his heart that took far too long to give up on her. The truth was, it never did.

A few diagnoses were made over the years, but only from a distance and always with the caveat that they were not binding, not official—Narcissistic Personality Disorder, Borderline Personality Disorder, Bipolar Disorder. She would never willingly be assessed, not after her stint in an institution when she was a youngster. Those records were sealed because of her age at the time. When she became an adult, the attitude of the experts was that unless someone wanted help, help could not be forced. Gone were the days when she could have been institutionalized. It would take an act of violence, and Oliver was not about to let the children fall victim. He also protected Mona from herself, at first. He alone was unprotected and had the scars, physical and emotional, as proof. No one could make Mona get help, and no one could protect her victims. Oliver understood little of the movement to deinstitutionalize the mentally ill, but he was sure he was not alone in cursing those who had instigated it without a plan in place for them or their families. Yes, there certainly were problems with the old system, the expense of such asylums being one of them, but did the pendulum have to swing so far to the other side? But who was he to voice such opinions? He had been a run-of-the-mill English professor albeit in a fine institution, but he was not a psychologist. All he had to go on was his own and his children's experiences, and he was working hard to forget the past, impossible as that was.

As the train made its rhythmic way out of the city, it passed graffiti-clad warehouses. One sixties-looking scrawl shouted out in neon orange and green, *Love is all you need.* Oliver wished for what must have been a young and inexperienced artist that the inscription was true. He had loved. He'd loved his children enough to sacrifice his life and happiness for them. He'd been astonished by love or what he thought was love when he'd first met Mona. The children had clamored for stories from a time before they had memory. Both were insistent, but Gwen seemed obsessed, so he'd told the story over and over, a watered-down, child-friendly version, of how he and their mother met. Telling the pair that their mother was not always the woman they knew helped keep Oliver sane. It didn't matter that the sweet and vulnerable woman he'd married lasted only about a month and showed up for short periods from time to time, just long enough to encourage hope. Often, it crossed his mind that his retelling of those few good early days may have kept the children looking for the different mother they'd hoped was hiding inside Mona. Telling such a tale may have been the best or the worst thing he could have done to them. He simply didn't know. Mona was stunningly beautiful—tall, graceful, intelligent. She remained all of those things, but his own idea of beauty had drastically altered over time and experience. That first encounter, though, nothing could erase a single moment of it from his memory.

Chapter 2

They'd met in Calgary at a conference of the Learned Society as it was so pretentiously called back then. Oliver was invited to give a presentation on the merits of names in the work of Margaret Laurence, a project he hoped to turn into a book. As always with these pompous gatherings, the room was stifling. The décor, heavy—burgundy drapes, gold and burgundy flocked wallpaper, tables over-burdened with layers of cloths and trays of food. The appetizers were fussy tidbits overworked by hands making too much contact with the ingredients. His appetite was never very good at these events. After the initial effrontery of the orientation room, Oliver looked around, hoping to recognize a colleague or plot his escape. He stopped at Mona who was holding a glass of red wine and looking straight at him. She was alone, and that was the first surprising thing he noticed. How could someone so beautiful not be surrounded by admirers? She smiled. At him. That was the second surprise.

Paralyzed, Oliver looked at her as though she were a hallucination sprung from a loneliness unrecognized until that moment. Although he was nearing forty, he was inexperienced, an introvert, and self-conscious around most women. Derek was the extrovert with his charming and easy-going ways. Oliver had spent most of his life reading, and those with whom he studied and worked were very much the same—scholarly introverts who would rather read about idealistic encounters than risk the attempt at one. Just a glance from Mona, and he could not move. He did not have to, for she came toward him, lowering her astonishingly beautiful blue eyes just as she came near.

"Looking for a way out of here?" she asked a little shyly and then laughed. She wore an electric-blue dress tailored to her slim build. Her dark hair was bobbed short, her bangs cut blunt. Everything about her was neat, tidy, and controlled, just the opposite of Oliver, a man ordinarily comfortable with his mismatched clothes, absent-mindedness, and awkward way of muddling through. In spite of her meticulous appearance, Oliver was aware of a vulnerability about Mona. Whether it was due to her slenderness or the pale skin of her unprotected neck when she dropped her gaze and dipped her head, he wasn't sure. The urge to put a protective arm around her was primal, but nervousness kept him in place.

"Watch out for this one."

Oliver was startled by the blond Adonis who'd joined them.

For one second, Mona, like an irritated cat, looked askance at the interloper. Gathering herself, she then smiled and stood back to introduce the two men.

"Oliver, meet Hewitt. Hewitt, Oliver. Hewitt is the head of the psychology department at our little institution. Ignore him, Oliver. All the women in the college are wise to Hewitt. He's just upset because none of us will give him the time of day."

Hewitt smiled and raised his glass to the two of them. "Don't say I didn't warn you," he nodded to Oliver and walked away.

Jackass, Oliver thought then turned his attention back to Mona who gave him all of hers. She was a sessional instructor in the English department at Eldon University College. It was a small college offering first and second-year university-equivalent courses. She'd been teaching there for two years and was in line to be tenured in another two.

When Oliver hesitantly said he was tenured at BCU, had been teaching there for years, and was giving a paper tomorrow at the conference, Mona put her hand on his arm and told him how wonderful it sounded. She insisted he tell her all about the paper, but not there in the suffocating room. They must leave and go somewhere quiet. Did he have his paper with him? Of course, he didn't. They'd have to go to his room where he could go over it with her. To give a paper at the Learned Society conference seemed the most magnificent thing in the world to her, or so he remembered her saying.

In minutes, Oliver felt like some kind of champion. All he needed was a white horse, and he could have ridden off with her, believing he had conquered the world. She tucked her arm in his and pressed so close to him he could feel her breast. Her hip wore against his as they walked to the door. Hewitt stood by the exit, glass in hand, discreetly shaking his head and smiling as she and Oliver, who refused to acknowledge that keeper of the gate, walked by.

That night ended as all such nights do, usually for people other than Oliver, for people about whom he'd only read or heard. Oliver awoke to Mona sleeping beside him, breath soft, and in her silent sleep she appeared so trusting, so innocent with her dark head cradled on the white pillow. He was still dazed by his luck, better than anything he had dreamed of or hoped for.

They'd gone over every detail of his paper—she was keenly interested. At times, her interest seemed a little over the top, but he brushed such thoughts away. She was a colleague and bound to be enthused by literature. When they were making love, she asked him to say her name, and he did. But she insisted that he say her full name. Mona was short for Desdemona, she insisted, and so he called out *Desdemona*, like some foolish student for the first time coming to *Othello*.

In the weak light of morning, he thought over her story. She had been hurt terribly by someone she would not name. Oliver knew it had to be Hewitt. The monster. It made sense, Hewitt warning him off, Hewitt standing at the door. He meant to intimidate both Oliver and Mona, but Oliver would put a stop to that. No more would that man lay a hand on her. She'd lost everything to him—he'd left after abusing her, after she'd threatened to call the police. She showed him the scar on her arm where she'd been cut by a mirror he'd thrown. He'd left and she hadn't the money to pay for their extravagant apartment, insisted upon by him. She hadn't known what to do. Should she have left his things and moved? Should she have paid what she could and stayed? She had been heartbroken, devastated. As she'd told Oliver these things, she shed tears. Not for the man, she insisted, but because of her own weakness.

"I felt so helpless," she said.

Oliver assured her it was not her fault.

"How could a grown woman get into such a situation?" she insisted.

Again, the blame was his, not hers, Oliver repeated.

Mona insisted on explaining even as Oliver said she did not have to. However, he wanted to hear just how far Hewitt had gone. The details fueled his anger.

She gave details—an eviction notice went up and the locks were changed. She couldn't get in to retrieve her belongings and had to begin all over again in a much humbler place. But that was all right. At least she was safe, she maintained, and didn't have to live in fear for her life.

All this she told him amid tears and little puffs of anger. Hook and all, he swallowed her story. Who would not, looking into those eyes? Who would not rush to her defense after touching her pale skin and embracing her frail body?

She had chosen well, chosen a brave man, a gullible one, a kind-hearted and loyal-to-a-fault hero who believed as truth every single one of her lies.

They were married at the end of the spring semester. It was a private affair with just a few friends and Mona's mother. His brother Derek could not come.

"I've got a huge presentation coming up. The biggest yet. If it's successful, I've got it made. Sorry, Ollie. I'd be there if I could," he said, and Oliver expressed disappointment but certainly understood.

The presentation must have been a success, for a few weeks later they received a check` from Derek for a ridiculous amount of money, more than two month's salary by Oliver's calculation. It would go a long way to increasing their savings. Mona's eyes lit up. Oliver felt obliterated from the scene as she danced around the room, check in hand singing, "Derek, lovely Derek."

Mona had a sister and brother, but she had not invited them to their wedding. She called them toxic and said she'd cut them out of her life.

"Are they bad people or mentally unstable?" he asked.

Startled, she turned on him and said, "Why would you ask that? Are you afraid there's something wrong with me, too?"

"Not at all. I simply wonder what kind of people they are that you would cut them out of your life so completely," he said, surprised at her vehemence.

Mona looked at him intently, as if gauging his unwariness. She must have decided that he was asking without guile so answered, "They hate me. They've always been jealous of me, and I am tired of their criticism, so I've cut them out of my life. End of story."

He decided not to question her about her name. It was Mona and not Desdemona. Their official documents said so. A small thing that did not warrant disrupting their day. A small thing that niggled in the back of his mind strongly enough to warn him to leave it alone but mark its significance. That she forgot the bridal bouquet of red roses in the registry office and told him not to bother going back for them had seemed to him heartless, but, he decided, she was simply being practical. They were not needed after the ceremony and would not have lasted beyond dinner at the restaurant.

Too late Oliver grasped the tragic flaw of the guileless, that they believe others to be as innocent and artless as they themselves.

Chapter 3

"Dinner is served," called the dining car steward. "Please come forward as your name is called."

Frequent travelers knew when meals were served on the train and had begun to gather in Oliver's car.

"Dr. Oliver Eastmund, Mr. and Mrs. McKenzie-Rae, Mr. Charles Amser, come this way, please."

Oliver stretched in his seat before attempting to stand. Time passed quickly in reverie, but his muscles were not about to forgive him such torpor. He stumbled with his first step, an old man, unsteady on his feet in the swaying car. Logical, reasonable. He must learn to pardon himself for these small things. How could he forgive the big things if he couldn't be kind to himself over this minor failing? The biggest failure of his life could never be forgiven, however.

He was surprised at the formal settings of the dining car—crisp white tablecloths, linen napkins, cutlery and glasses that competed to outshine each other. A little vase of Peruvian lilies. In a word, the space looked elegant beyond his expectations.

"Dr. Eastmund, you are at table nine," the steward said.

Oliver thanked him and walked down the car to his appointed table, the McKenzie-Raes and Charles Amser closely following.

"You're a doctor," Julia McKenzie-Rae said after they were seated and introductions made.

"Not a medical doctor," Oliver said. "Ph.D. I am, or was, an English professor. Retired now." He'd forgotten not to identify himself as Dr. Eastmund when he'd bought his ticket. He'd have to work on dropping that habit if he didn't want to repeatedly explain himself. Oliver was not attached to the title nor was he defined by it. He'd have a word with the steward after dinner.

"Julia and I are going across Canada. We're stopping for a few days in places along the way—Jasper, Saskatoon, Winnipeg, Toronto, Kingston..." Roger McKenzie-Rae continued their litany of stops all the way to Halifax.

"You'll be traveling for some time," Oliver said, comfortable enough with this small talk.

Julia answered, "We've got no time limit. We've just retired, and we're going to see the country."

Oliver smiled at her enthusiasm. He searched her face just long enough to avoid being rude. She seemed sane, but how could you tell? He reminded himself that his wife was a rarity, that most women were not like Mona.

"I'm off to Toronto to see my son and daughter. I may move there if I like the place and my children don't mind having me around," he said. He emphasized *I, me* and *my* enough that the Mackenzie-Raes understood not to ask about a Mrs. Eastmund who might move to Toronto as well.

"What about you, Mr. Amser? Where are you off to?" Julia said.

"Business trip to Thunder Bay," Charles Amser said and went back to eating his savory tart, finished with conversation.

After dinner, Oliver returned to his car. Each meal would give him the opportunity to speak with new people, but as polite as he would be, he would keep them at arm's length. At this point, a new friend would be burdensome, and he was shedding burdens, not acquiring them. His reminiscences were heavy enough. He hoped he'd brought sufficient changes of clothes that would be appropriate for the more formal dining on the train. He had become accustomed to keeping up appearances and would handle this situation although dog-tired from the effort of putting on a good front.

A book in hand to guard against unwanted conversation, Oliver gazed at the window. All was black without, and the only thing he could see was his own dim reflection. Unfortunately, the train took them through the mountains at night, depriving the passengers of spectacular views. The others would likely see them on their return trip. But he would not be returning by train.

Many of the passengers gathered in the hospitality car to play bridge or work on puzzles. He would avoid that crowd and get a cup of coffee later. For now, he stayed put and hid behind his book.

As passengers left their games and pastimes, some walked through his car on the way to their own and nodded to Oliver as they went by. He stretched back in his seat to see if the coast was clear, but the hospitality car was not yet empty. He'd wait even though waiting with little to occupy himself might lead him to reminisce. *In time*, he told himself, *these thoughts will dissipate in time.*

Oliver picked up his book and read the same paragraph he had covered three times since he'd first sat down. Not a word was getting through. Staring into an open book gave him some protection from the intrusion of others on board but not from his recollections. He read aloud under his breath but felt the eyes of some of the passing passengers on him, a dotty old man muttering to himself. He took a pencil out of his backpack and ticked each line as he read as much to help him focus on the story he was reading as to keep his mind from wandering. It worked for a short while until he caught himself staring at a sentence not ticking it off, the pencil poised. Like a movie, memories played before him.

Chapter 4

About a month after their wedding, Mona, who'd taken on two summer courses to teach, announced her pregnancy.

"I thought you were on the pill," he said. Until that moment, one he wished he could skip back and redo, they'd been sitting comfortably in the living room, she with a pile of marking on the coffee table, and he reading a book. It wasn't as if he was unhappy about the turn of events. He thought she was going to focus on her career for the next few years, until she was tenured, at least. This is what she'd claimed.

"You don't want this baby?" She turned her head slowly and looked at him with narrowed eyes, a rabid animal ready to spring.

He did not recognize this woman. He was not prepared for what was to come.

She threw down the paper she was marking and jumped to her feet. "Shall I have an abortion, then?" she screamed. "I'll get rid of it if that's your attitude." She spat the words, spat at him.

Baffled, he got up to embrace her and explain himself.

"I'll get rid of myself while I'm at it, and that should make you happy."

He had no opportunity to correct himself, no chance to get a word in before she began pummeling him with her fists.

"You bastard. You son of a bitch. You've never wanted me, and now you don't want this baby. I hate you." She stopped hitting him long enough to lift and smash the vase his department had given them as a wedding gift. The crystal exploded. Shards flew across the room.

Oliver covered his head and turned away. Her fists beat at his spine and shoulders. Not once did he think to hit her back. Not once did he think to hold her wrists to stop the blows. Before he could act, she grabbed her keys, ran to the car, and squealed out of the driveway. What was he supposed to do? She didn't have her purse or her phone. He couldn't call her. She was wild in her anger. What was he to do?

An hour later, after cleaning up the glass and pacing the living room then calling a few people he thought she might know, Oliver decided to call her mother. He barely knew the woman, meeting her once at their wedding. He explained Mona's outburst to Frances. He told her he thought it was perhaps because of hormonal imbalance due to her pregnancy.

"She's pregnant? Good lord." After a long pause, Frances sighed and said, "I wondered how long it would take."

"What do you mean, Frances?" he asked, wrong in assuming she was referring to the pregnancy.

"You must have noticed, Oliver. Mona is not...well. She is not like other people."

"You're scaring me, Frances. What are you talking about?"

"Mona has these...moods. She's had them all her life. We tried to help her, her father and I, but nothing worked. She was briefly institutionalized as a youngster because we didn't need her consent. As she got older, there was nothing we could do. She refused to take her medication, said it made her feel groggy and slow. She would be fine for a month or two but then spiral out of control. It's not her fault. She didn't ask for this, but it's just how it is."

"Frances, what was the diagnosis? What is wrong with her?"

"I can't recall, Oliver. It was all gobbledygook to me. It was so long ago."

A long stretch of silence, during which he tried to connect the woman he loved and married with the daemon he had earlier witnessed, ended with Frances saying she would call him if Mona contacted her.

He hung up and waited.

Chapter 5

"I'll make up your berth now, sir." The porter apologized for disturbing him. Oliver shook off his cumbersome thoughts, thanked him, and grabbed his suitcase. He headed for the shower room. Oliver stood swaying under the running water. He knew he couldn't stay long, had to consider other passengers and their needs, but for just a few more minutes he unwound in the steaming shower wishing for all he was worth that he could wash the memories away like so much dirt. The years had been dirty—filthy, ugly, dragged-in-the-mud laundry—but he could not rinse the memories clean. He dried off and looked warily at his face in the mirror, expecting to see guilt personified. But it was a sad and weary face although a little hope lingered about the eyes. He would begin a new life soon, with Gavin and Theresa and with Gwendolyn. He returned to his berth in his pajamas and heavy bathrobe, tucked his suitcase away, then stepped through to the hospitality car.

"Well, now, here's a man who's done this before," a woman said. She was similarly attired and sitting at a table drinking a cup of tea.

Oliver focused on stirring his coffee. There was no one else in the car. He could not avoid a conversation.

"No," he finally replied, "I usually fly." He turned, cup in hand, and looked at her. She was much older than he, not a damsel in distress, not a shrinking violet, that was certain. She looked a little on the tough side with a voice to match. She wore no makeup and her short hair was wild and spiked and naturally gray. Oliver had a practiced cautiousness about making judgments based upon appearances. He felt she may be a no-nonsense practical person who, if she did not have all the answers to life's mysteries, would give her best-educated guess but only if asked. Aside from the toughness, she reminded him of his mother, a down-to-earth, reliable sort of woman. Early on, he'd come to expect all women to be that way, but he'd learned through experience, bitter and damaging, it was not true. If his mother had been less forthright, less dependable, more manipulative, would he have learned to tell the difference? Would he have been prepared for life to be as insane as his had been? He had no answer. Leave it to the psychologists, to the Hewitts of the world to figure out.

Oliver sat down across from her. He used his napkin to wipe up the coffee he spilled as the train rocked. "You'd think I'd have my sea-legs by now," he said.

"Just wait until you try to get to sleep tonight," the woman offered. "The whole damn train will feel like it's going to tip off the tracks, it sways so much. Here," she said as she offered him one of the cookies she had piled on the table.

He nodded his thanks as he took a bite.

"Game of blackjack?" she asked as she pushed a pack of cards toward him. "The name's Shirley. I'm headed for Montreal. Who are you?"

Just as he thought. She was straightforward and refreshingly blunt. He responded in kind. "Yes, as long as no money is involved. I'm Oliver, and I'm off to Toronto to see my kids."

He opened the deck of cards and began to shuffle. "I haven't played this in a long while," he said keeping the conversation light. He'd played cards with the children when they were young, but they rarely finished a few hands. Always invited to play, Mona invariably refused at first then chose to join in after the game was well underway. More often than not, she'd stomp off, or worse, claim they were cheating and ganging up on her if she lost. It was the same with any board game with one exception. "My game is chess." Mona should have been a master at the game given her propensity for manipulation. Perhaps because on the board her moves could be seen and more easily anticipated, she loathed the game and would never play. Chess became a regular pursuit for Oliver, Gavin, and Gwendolyn.

"My kids loved chess so much that when they moved away from home, they legally changed their last name to Rook," Oliver said. He gave a little laugh and slapped down an ace of hearts. She was a woman who invited confidences. Sure he would never see her again after this trip, he spoke to her as if he were reinforcing the details of his life. He supposed he should be more parsimonious with information, but what harm could it do now?

"Didn't that bother you, them changing their name, dropping yours?" Shirley asked.

"Not at all. I encouraged them to do it. They were starting a new life and wanted nothing to do with the old. I couldn't blame them. The past was not going to be allowed to haunt them." He would have to be careful, however. Not too many details.

"Geeze, what'd they do, rob a bank or something?" Shirley threw down a nine of spades to add to her two fives and won the hand.

"No, nothing like that. My wife was…ill…and they spent their childhood living under that shadow. They had to grow up much too fast, and I'm sure they were simply trying to shed those difficult times and have some freedom. In fact, I'm going to change my name as well. Oliver Rook. It has a certain ring to it, don't you think?"

Shirley looked at him and shrugged. "It sounds okay, but Eastmund isn't bad either. 'A rose by any other name'…" Shirley looked straight into his eyes. "Seems a shame to have to go through all that trouble."

With more than a hint of sarcasm, he said, "Trouble? You have no idea." He stopped himself then added. "Let's leave it at that, shall we? I've got to win a few hands or be skunked."

He won the second hand and the third. Shirley won the rest of the ten rounds in all.

"Thanks for the entertainment," she said as she packed up the deck of cards.

"You mean the slaughter." He grinned as he took both mugs to the sink.

"Goodnight, then."

"I hope it will be."

Shirley headed toward her berth as Oliver wiped crumbs from the table then moved in the opposite direction toward his car.

It was a difficult night. As Shirley predicted, the train swayed precariously as it sped along. In the cramped quarters of his berth, he couldn't hold a book steady enough to read. His eyes tried to cling to a line of words, but the lurching made him queasy, so he laid down the collection of stories and put in his ear buds to listen to one of his audiobooks. He shut off the light, and soon the reader's soothing voice made him drowsy. He fell asleep listening to a sultry rendition of *Tender is the Night*.

The train pitched violently back and forth. Oliver's head hit the window ledge. Startled awake, he sat up and instinctively covered his face. It took him a second to get his bearings. Unmoored in the pre-dawn light, he eventually allowed himself the luxury of feeling rocked and comforted by the swaying of the car. He knew he was a beaten man. It was enough to make him give one big moan, unheard above the rumble of the train. Except for tears in his eyes as he rubbed sleep from them, he managed to control himself. It would take some time to trust this new freedom and to lay down his arms. But not yet. He would have to play things out to the end. In the swaying car, his thoughts returned to Mona.

Chapter 6

Five-year-old Gwen, her long hair blonde against her flower-printed nightgown, waited in the hallway at the entrance to the kitchen. She was close enough to hear them but far enough away to be out of danger. She stood with her arms slightly bent as if ready to protect herself. Oliver tried to keep his expression blank as Mona screamed about their canceled Holt Renfrew credit card, the last one she had and the one she had hidden from him until the bailiff came to the door to collect. They were desperately in debt. Mona would not or could not curb her spending. It was part of her disorder, the therapist he had consulted explained. Not only had Oliver canceled all of their credit cards, he'd sent registered letters to each company insisting that Mona not be issued replacement cards at any time, that he would not be responsible for her debts, this on the expensive advice of a lawyer. He could have declared bankruptcy, but that seemed to him a dishonorable act for a man who had a profession that would most likely last long enough to pay the debt, her debt. It was his cross to bear. The price of impetuousness.

Oliver was a master at keeping a calm face. He remained motionless as he spoke evenly and soothingly. "We've talked about this, Mona. Our finances are shot."

He assumed a familiar posture, aware and ready to stop Mona from hurting him or herself.

Mona threw up her hands, her fingers rigid and spread wide. She shook them menacingly close to his face as she screamed incoherently in her rage. Oliver stayed neutral. Mona, her teeth bared, lips pulled back tightly, looked grotesque. Spittle flecked her chin. In horrifyingly slow increments, she began to crouch.

Oliver looked over toward Gwen for a split second to reassure her that everything would be all right.

Mona sprang.

With a practiced step, Oliver moved back and raised his hands to protect his face. She reached for his eyes. Oliver grabbed her wrists and held her away. He could not stop her penetrating screams or her kicks to his already bruised shins. He looked back to Gwen, but she was gone, back to her room without a word. He hoped she had locked her door as he had taught her.

In that moment, Mona bit his hand, drawing blood and a cry from Oliver, which satisfied her enough to laugh. He pushed her further away and she crowed victoriously. She had hurt him, and that was what she was after.

"You think you can beat me?" she snarled as she slunk back into her room. "I'll get what I want one way or another."

Oliver knew that was true, but he'd had little choice. They could barely cover rent and utilities. It was always a toss-up as to what would be paid—electricity or gas, Wi-Fi and phone or rent. He put aside money each pay for the children's expenses for school and sports. Both he and Mona could make that small sacrifice whether Mona agreed or not. What she didn't know wouldn't hurt her or him.

But what was certainly hurting Gavin and Gwendolyn was being witness to Mona's shocking attacks. How many times had his children watched these dramas? How long before they were no longer shocking but accepted as normal behavior? Out of fear for their emotional development, he had left with the children once. But she was brilliant and beautiful and could manipulate like Satan himself. She was no lawyer, but in a courtroom, she convinced a judge to sign an injunction to have the children returned to her. Oliver would never leave them. He hired lawyers to fight for full custody, but she was masterful at disguising her insanity. She refused to go for treatment, so no official diagnosis of her condition existed except for his testimony. She played the role of the poor, mistreated woman convincingly, sobbing loudly, flinching every time he spoke up for himself, and looking at the judge with those eyes that could, instantaneously, seem for all the world like those of a lamb being sent to slaughter, pleading for salvation. His record of taking the children from their mother was used against him time and again, and he was smart enough not to continue along this foolish path. He could lose them forever. He stayed to face the dragon.

There was no help available for him or for the children. No agency was equipped to monitor Mona, and even if one could be found, she had the ability to behave as if she were sane for as long as needed, if she were being watched.

It was all a play to her, a play in which she had the starring role and the rest of the actors were there simply to revolve around her.

However, she'd almost made a mistake or two in her methodical plans to keep them under her control. Gavin was eight, Gwendolyn just six. Oliver woke one morning to Mona shouting at the children, pounding on their bedroom doors and screaming for them to get up. It was not yet light. Oliver, who slept in his office, ran down the hall to reach them.

"What's wrong, Mona," he said, keeping his voice calm. The children cried, frightened out of sleep.

"These two," she shouted, "these two left a mess in the bathroom. Toothpaste all over the sink, water on the counter." Mona was livid.

Oliver stood between her and the children's doors lowering his voice and slowing the pace. "They can clean it up in the morning before they go to school. Let them get some sleep. It's early yet." As always, his attempts to intervene caused outrage. Mona shouted at the top of her lungs, confused threats and accusations.

"Mona, please take your medication. You are over-excited." Although the only pills she had, that he knew of, were for anxiety, and they had never worked to dissuade her from these terrible episodes, he made the suggestion out of concern for her but more because it would redirect her fury to him and away from the children. He moved her from the hallway into the living room by taking steps backward as she laid into him. He turned on a lamp, keeping his eyes on her as she circled around him. The curtains were open though he had closed them before he went to bed. Mona must have been up looking for some way to vent her rising agitation before taking aim at the children. In the dimness, he caught sight of their neighbor, Mrs. White, walking her dog early in the dark morning. She was watching them.

Mona, with her back to the window and unaware of their audience, upped the decibels of her rant and raised both fists to begin her assault. But she stopped. She caught him looking beyond her, through the window. She turned, saw Mrs. White, and flew to the window, pulling the curtains together, but not before she gave their neighbor the finger.

"Thought you had a witness. She won't be any help to you." Mona charged toward him. Oliver crossed his arms in front of his face and took the full force of her attack on his chest. Only when she picked up a bronze statuette did he reach for her wrists to keep her from using it as a weapon. She kicked him and tried to bite his arm, but he was ready for her.

Gavin came out in the hall shouting, "Stop it, Mama. Stop it."

Oliver said in as steady a voice as Mona's thrashing would allow, "Go back to your room, son, and lock the door." That was all he could say before Mona broke one fist free and hit him in the mouth. Again, he grabbed hold of her wrists, the taste of blood on his tongue.

Mrs. White must have called the police, for in an instant, red and blue flashing lights shone on the living room drapes as cars pulled up. Oliver opened the curtains with one hand while holding Mona back with the other. Mrs. White was outside with an officer and two others walked up to the house. Oliver let Mona go. She made a swing at him and caught him hard on the left temple. The blow made him dizzy. Had they seen? Had they witnessed her hitting him? He staggered to the door to let the officers in. No sooner had the police stepped over the threshold than Mona began sobbing her usual tale of abuse. This time, however, they had the neighbor's account of at least the beginning of Mona's actions. But had they seen Mona hit him?

Even in his stunned and embarrassed state, Oliver saw the chance for a way out. A charge of assault against Mona would be a way to crack open the door to full custody of the children. He told the officers to lay charges.

"Look, buddy," the older cop, one who looked like he was on the verge of retirement, said. "No one saw her hit you, so it's your word against hers. You're going to have a hard time charging her. Look at her. No judge in the world is going to convict that tiny thing of assault." His partner, a young rookie, opened his mouth to protest, but the older officer stopped him.

"Look at my face," Oliver pleaded, touching his temple and tasting again the blood on his lip. "She doesn't have a mark on her. Just look at her, at both of us." Oliver had not a drop of anger to motivate him. The cold and certain spread of inevitability reached up through his legs and body and gripped his chest. He would never be free. He could never leave the children. He had no choice. Useless as his entreaty was, he turned to the rookie officer who had looked like he wanted to help. Oliver said again, he wanted to press charges.

"Don't look at him. I'm in charge here," said the older cop. "You don't have a leg to stand on, buddy. We can't lay charges on something nobody but you saw."

He did not say it out loud, did not want to give Mona any ideas, but he knew if things were reversed, if she were the one to say he had hit her, had shown the cut lip and the swelling temple, he'd be in handcuffs before he could say a word. But the law, just like every authority he had dealt with, was biased. Nothing came of his plea.

"Not going to happen, buddy. Kiss and make up. It'll all blow over." The young officer cringed but was too inexperienced to argue with his senior in command. Times were changing but not for the officer in charge or quickly enough for Oliver.

Oliver watched them leave. He could choke her to death, but where would that leave the children? Frances was too old to care for them. His parents were gone. There was Derek, his brother, who was as wild and free-spirited as Oliver was constrained, who had said to him, "Get your head out of your ass," when he touched on the subject of his plight with Mona. Besides, Derek wasn't married, had a string of girlfriends, and changed locations as often as he changed his mind. No, Derek couldn't handle the responsibility. Besides, they hadn't seen much of each other since he'd accused Mona of coming on to him.

He called his lawyer the next day, but the costs to fight for sole custody in such a case were horrendous. They were so in debt and the retainer alone was in the thousands.

"It will be an uphill battle," the lawyer explained. "And there's no guarantee things won't go the other way. It all depends on the judge and how convincing you are as opposed to your wife."

He had his answer. Beauty was more convincing than truth. He was a fool trapped by exquisite evil.

A cycle of quietness pervaded the house after Mona's blow-ups. He could not call the mood peaceful or even calm because all of them were tense waiting for the next round. But from time to time, she would surprise them. Mona's placidity could last for long stretches—a month or a little more—long enough for the children to reach out to her for whatever morsel of affection she might offer, long enough for a tiny seed of hope to germinate in the aggregate of wariness that rooted Oliver. These were untroubled days, and short as they were, they were days that fed his optimism. They were also days during which silent static built up to the next explosive episode.

Too often, during those quiet days, she'd beg his forgiveness. "I know there's something wrong with me. I'll get help, I promise."

Even before the children were born, how many times had he heard this? How many times was he supposed to forgive her madness and hold out until she made good on her word? A lifetime, apparently, but she never did get the help she promised to find. Even when he found it for her, she refused.

"Dr. Morris is an expert, Mona. Read his books. He's compassionate. He understands. He's not out to lay blame."

In the quiet times, in the aftermath of lovemaking, she would agree to see a therapist. She would caress Oliver, her hero, her gentle knight and kiss away his fears. But always, she made one excuse after another until the next blow-up. But the times in between kept him hopeful and hooked.

Chapter 7

He could not sleep. At four-thirty, Oliver got up and put on his robe and slippers. He went to the hospitality car and made a full pot of coffee and a few slices of toast. It would be hours before breakfast proper appeared in the dining car and with it a table of strangers for whom he would need to put on a good front. He loved early mornings, even this one in spite of his rough night.

The car was spotless. The night before, Oliver noted the mess of the room—dirty mugs left on tables and the counter, games left unfinished. It had smelled like someone sneaked an illicit cigarette or two, and it smelled like all closed-in spaces—stale and musty. Before he'd left last night, he shut off the video that played continuously in the background, concerned it might disturb those in berths nearest the hospitality car. Sometime during the night, the crew must have scrubbed the place clean and opened a window although all of them seemed tightly sealed. Either that or Oliver was becoming used to life in this enclosed tube on wheels.

The car was empty. No one stirred. No one, unfortunately, to interrupt his thoughts when they turned to the rare beautiful days he'd had with Mona. He fought against those memories. They reminded him of his powerlessness, of his own weakness, of his culpability. He'd rather churn up the rage—both hers and his. How could he live out the rest of his life if, in these quiet mornings, all he could remember were her beauty and the gentle, remorseful side of her that begged his forgiveness, begged for his help, and promised love and serenity?

"Hello, Oliver." Shirley interrupted his thoughts in her husky voice, a voice even more gravelly in the morning than it had been the night before.

Oliver looked at her over his shoulder and smiled. "Coffee's ready. We're the first customers." His toast popped, and he offered the slices to her.

"You go ahead. I'll make my own."

Oliver sat at the same table they had occupied yesterday and sighed with relief.

"We'll be in Kamloops soon. Supposed to arrive at six A.M. if the train is on time, which it is," Shirley said as she looked at her watch.

"How many times have you made this trip?" he asked.

"Oh, about a dozen or so since I retired. I have family and friends in Montreal and more in Vancouver, so I split my time between the two. I've got nothing else to do. By the way, did you get any sleep last night? Things were rocking and rolling pretty hard." Shirley chuckled.

"I was fine until I hit my head. No harm done, though I did think we'd go off the rails at one point. Is it always like this?"

"No, just through the mountains. You'll feel better about this stretch when you come back. The view is spectacular."

"I don't plan to come back, Shirley. I hope to stay in Toronto."

"Sold your house and belongings, did you? No friends or family to bring you back?"

"As I said, my children are in Toronto. My friends were all work colleagues, and I'm retired now. There is nothing for me to go back to." He knew he sounded convincing since it was the truth. He would have to contend with the belongings in the house he and Mona rented from the university, but that would have to wait. She was the sole occupant now, and he winced at the thought. He would not go back to face that until he had to. He'd fly there when the time came.

"You're free as a bird," she said. "It's a great feeling, isn't it?"

Oliver peered into her eyes. Was it wisdom he saw there and insight or was she simply prying? She looked straight into his, smiled, and raised her mug to him before taking a sip. Oliver raised his to her and gave her a half smile before looking away.

He dressed long before breakfast was announced at eight thirty. Seated with another group of strangers, Oliver made small talk about the weather, destinations, and the trip in general, careful not to create the opportunity for friendship or confidences. He left the dining car as soon as he was finished.

Rain streaked across the windows blurring the landscape. The day was interrupted by a few stops—Clearwater then Blue River. Near one o'clock, lunch was served after their stop in Valemount. A quiet young couple whose attitude bordered on morose joined him and an equally silent older man at table. Few words other than a comment or two on the cuisine passed between them, and that suited Oliver. As soon as he could politely leave, he stood to go back to his car. Painfully aware of becoming stiff with inertia, he would have to come up with a plan to get some exercise, preferably activity that would keep his mind from dwelling on the past. For now, he settled down to read or perhaps doze off for a short while. Anything to pass the interminable hours.

Chapter 8

In hindsight, evidence of just how off the wall she was, was obvious even before Gavin's birth. On the Monday Oliver returned to teach after a week off caring for her with her dreadful morning sickness, Mona's phone calls increased. Calling him frequently was something she'd done since they'd started seeing each other. She'd call, just once or twice a day at first, and for a while the attention was wonderful. But her more frequent calls eventually got tiresome and he ignored one or two. Yet he did not see this as a hint of something worse. After they were married, she called even more. She was checking up on him, he was sure of it. He would sit at his desk in his office and count her calls. Ten, fifteen. They were incessant. Students often complained that they could not get through to him, and he tried to explain this to her. It was something she should be aware of, having been an instructor herself. By the time she left work claiming disability due to a problematic pregnancy, her own diagnosis, the calls became threatening and abusive.

"I'm going to kill myself. You have to come home. I can't go through with this pregnancy." Three months pregnant with Gavin was the first time she did this. He ran like a madman from his office to their home just off campus, terrified, convinced he'd find her on the floor with wrists slashed. When he arrived, she lay naked on the living room couch, batting her eyes at him, a salacious grin smudged across her face. He was stunned. He'd raced home, barely avoiding being hit by a car, his heart pounding, terrified. He hadn't called the police or an ambulance—he hadn't thought of it. His only thought was to get home. It was his turn to be furious, but she gave him little room to express his anger. She turned on him.

"Now that you've got me knocked up, you can't stand to look at me, can you."

And the fight began. His blood pounded in his ears, so he could only hear the odd word—insensitive, betrayal, coward, hateful—thrown into the argument with little connection to logic, truth, or reality. While he could take her blows, he feared for the baby, especially when she began to beat her abdomen with her fists, screaming that she hated it. If only he had called the police at that moment. If only he had thought to bring someone with him as a witness. She might have been committed at least for a short time. There would have been a record of her insanity. But he hadn't. With his limited experience, he was sure he was all the things she called him. He was convinced he was doing something wrong. Marriage was not supposed to be like this, was it? His naked, pregnant wife screaming at him, beating him, beating herself, their unborn baby?

He wrapped his arms around her, and in spite of the strength her rage gave her, he held her close to his chest. She had to tire at some point. She couldn't keep this up forever. She tried to slip through his arms and drop to the floor, but he held on. She kicked and screamed and tried to bite his chest through his wool jacket but could not. He kept her in his embrace. He clenched her close until her screams turned to child-like sobs that shook through him. He hung on even when in exhaustion her body slumped and her sobs became whimpers. He carried her to their bed, and instead of letting him go when he laid her down, she clung to him like a frightened child. She seemed so much like one—terrified of her own actions, frightened of herself. At moments like this, she came close to being as honest as she could about who and what she was—terrified that he would leave her and she would be alone, horrified at the monster she had become.

Oliver read book upon book on every disorder suggested. In spite of the often-contradictory advice, he tried their suggestions of being attentive, supportive, reassuring. They helped him cope, somewhat, by informing him that he was not the cause of her behavior, but no matter how hard he tried, he could not control her outbursts or help her.

Three more times during her pregnancy with Gavin, Mona threatened suicide, but her mother had been with her once and reassured Oliver that her threat was empty. One time, he showed up with a colleague, Brenda Macintyre, and as controlled as Mona was while Brenda was there, the cost to him while they were alone was high.

"Why did you bring her with you," Mona threw at him once Brenda had assured herself that Mona was all right and left.

"I had little choice, Mona. Brenda was in the room when you called, and I accidentally hit speaker. She heard every word you uttered. What did you expect, making the threat you did? She insisted on driving me. It was faster than running."

"You told her. I know you did."

"Told her what? What was I supposed to have told her, that you're hysterical? That you've lost your mind?" He thought she would lunge at him for that comment, but she seemed oblivious to it. Her sudden silence put him on guard.

As the idea dawned on her, she said, "You're having an affair with her and you're trying to get me out of the picture." She half smiled at him, a wicked, bitter smile.

"For God's sake, Mona," he protested. "I'm not having an affair. I don't have the time or energy for an affair."

She turned away from him as she said, "So, you're saying you would if you had the time. That's good to know. That's reassuring." She swung around, her fist clenched ready to strike. Rage gave her frightening strength, and Oliver was at the receiving end of every word, every punch, every well-aimed kick, claw, and slash.

The third time Mona called to say she was going to kill herself she left a voice message since he'd stopped answering her calls. He was, in truth, teaching a class at the time. When he finally got the message, it was two hours later. He did not rush home. He did not say a word about her message that evening when he got back but waited for her to bring it up. The accusations flew, but not about the meaningless threat she'd made. She was furious that he had not answered his phone and had not at least called her back.

It took everything he had not to respond with sarcasm. On the tip of his tongue was, *What happened? Didn't take enough poison? Did the rope break? Run out of pills, did you?* Although he thought these things, he did not say them. He did not add fuel to her conflagration. He let her wear herself out, but he, too, was being worn down, his empathy unraveling, his personality changing. He, too, was imprisoned by her insanity.

Over the years, her moments of calm and remorse became rarer and hard won. They never brought Mona to the point where she would go for help. Always, always they ended up with her begging him to make love to her, and he would comply. In the back of his mind, he knew he was doing little but feeding the madness but he could not bring himself to add to her fears by walking away. Not then, when he still had hope. When he still had love. And, of course, later, there were the children. Never would he leave them.

Chapter 9

The train stopped in Jasper at four o'clock. Oliver nodded to the couple who settled in the seats across the aisle from him then buried his face in his book in hopes they would not try to strike up a conversation. So often, people interrupted readers to relieve them of boredom, equating reading with doing nothing. He prayed they were not that kind. Briefly, Oliver thought of leaving the train to walk around the station. There was plenty of time, but it was a small building, and no one was tempted to step out into the dimness and the downpour. The only things worth seeing were the hanging flower baskets decorating the station. They were huge, and from his seat he counted eight. Probably more around the front, all of them overflowing with the last of the season's blooms. Trailing red petunias, white alyssum, crimson geraniums, blue lobelia, as well as ivy. Red, orange, burgundy, and yellow tufts of celosia. Whoever maintained them was doing a great job, for even in the waxing autumn, the gloom of late afternoon, and through the veil of rain, they radiated color and cheer. Their intensity reminded him of his own garden, a beautiful refuge for the three of them until Gavin and Gwendolyn left.

He had spent much of his time in the garden with the children since he could not afford to take them far on vacation, not that bringing Mona places would be anything short of disastrous. The children spent most of the summer at swimming lessons and splashing around in the community pool. The lessons served them well, for they'd both earned lifeguard certificates before leaving home. But camping for a week or two during the summers was their vacation of choice.

Mona would not go with them.

"Why should I go camping and have to do all the work without the conveniences of home? It's not my idea of a vacation."

At first, he'd looked at her in disbelief when she uttered such words. She did nothing at home except complain about the way he and the children kept house. If she had to make a meal for herself, she considered it a great imposition.

"I want to go someplace warm, stay in a hotel, and let others wait on me."

"We can't afford it," he answered each time, avoiding the obvious. "Camping is the most we can do on our budget. You'll have to get a job if you'd like to go somewhere warm."

Those were fighting words.

Each March break, the three of them sat at the computer to plan a new spot for their summer retreat. The dry, desert-like interior, the mountainous regions north of the city, or one of the many Salish Sea islands. Oliver, Gwen and Gavin would pitch a tent and rise and sleep in rhythm with nature, the only scolding coming from crows and whiskey jacks.

If they could not afford a luxurious vacation far away, then he could try to make their backyard a place of beauty. He drew up plans for borders and raised beds that would incorporate flowers as well as vegetables and fruit. Planning and implementing were two different things, however—one cheap, the other expensive. Nevertheless, with Gwen and Gavin under foot, Oliver dug into the hard-packed earth, removing clumps of sod and working the soil until, fine as sand, it ran through his fingers. One by one, the neighbors, who came out to speak with him while he worked, offered him plants divided from their own perennials or extra seedlings they had begun indoors in the late winter. From them, Oliver learned the knack for sprouting his own seeds in a south-facing basement window. Some he exchanged with his neighbors in the planting season. The three researched and learned to compost kitchen scraps and create ecologically-friendly repellents for pests that threatened their produce. Summer evenings, they ate out of doors, barbecuing on an improvised steel drum Oliver rescued from the alley and repurposed.

Mona refused to eat anything cooked on his homemade contraption. "You don't know what was in that thing," she complained. "As if I'd eat off something pulled from the trash."

Although he tried repeatedly to explain it was an old cooking-oil drum that had been scrubbed clean and certainly sterilized by fire, Oliver could not reason with her. He tried with all sincerity, but the truth was that dinners outdoors with the children were preferable to eating with Mona, as much as he knew he should be trying harder to include her in their meals and in their lives. He was aware she had little interest in them except to keep the three of them within her grasp, hostages, for as long as she could. If she'd only given them some encouragement, a scrap of hope, they would have embraced her fully and openly—they needed her desperately—but she parceled-out crumbs of love as if it were medicine to keep the family barely alive but not strong enough to thrive.

Year after year, the garden improved. He received peach and apple saplings from Mrs. White who often encouraged Oliver as he built up the patch. Mr. Spitalari, who lived behind them, gave him six raspberry canes that produced so many berries the second year, they were able to freeze batches and enjoy their red richness throughout the winter. Oliver learned how to can applesauce and peaches. He froze peas and green beans, spinach and kale. From the Krestics who lived two doors down, he learned how to store carrots and potatoes so they would last well into the next year. Gwen became quite proficient at flower arranging, and she brought bouquets of giant marigolds, daisies, rudbeckia and Russian sage to her teachers. She would make bouquets for her mother who complained about the scent of the marigolds and placed them outside on the picnic table. The only scent Mona could abide was that of roses, so Gavin and Oliver planted red, white, pink, and coral-colored roses whose blossoms Gwen made into sweet bouquets that Mona kept to herself in her room.

The garden was a joy for Oliver and the children. Sometimes Mona, on her good days, would sit out and read on the small patch of lawn near the porch. On those days, Oliver would not start the barbecue but cooked indoors to let Mona and the children enjoy their rare pleasant time together.

"You're becoming a little Suzy homemaker, aren't you?" Her snide remark made as he canned the last of the tomatoes one evening in late September.

He laughed at the comment. It was true. He was certainly doing things he never in his life thought he would do—canning, gardening, cooking, cleaning—all these things he did because she wouldn't, of course, but also because he discovered he liked the idea of growing and preserving the food his family ate. He had lived alone before Mona, and he knew how to keep house. He liked the home he provided for his family to be clean and tidy. He had no expectations that Mona should be the one to do it, no resentment that she didn't. He simply did what had to be done to live the way he felt they should live.

"*Little House on the Prairie* in here. You're more Ma than Pa. Some man you are," she pushed, not satisfied with his lack of anger and retaliation. "Maybe we should invite some friends over to sample your culinary expertise."

"Friends?" he responded. "What friends do you have in mind? What friends do we have? You've closed the door on that front." He knew he should just let her barbs fly over him, but he was tired and hot and not feeling particularly noble.

"Well, I've got friends. I've got one friend in particular, and he doesn't spend his time acting like some kind of quintessential housewife. He's a man, a real man."

He knew she meant Hewitt.

When the train started again, Oliver walked the narrow aisles to get some exercise before dinner. As the cars rocked, no longer did he feel confined but was grateful for those constricting halls that held him up. He could not afford one of the private cabins that lined some carriages. After peering in one or two of the open doors, he was glad he opted for a berth—a seat by day and a bed by night. It was much more open. He could not picture spending any time at all in a confined cabin with Mona. One or the other of them would be dead early into a journey, he most likely.

In a short time, he would have spent twenty-four hours on the train. He decided to call home when he returned to his seat. As he knew it would be, the conversation was one-sided as he spoke to the answering machine.

"Hello. It's me. I've just left Jasper and it's pouring rain. Can't see a thing. I hope you are well and keeping busy. Any plans for tomorrow? Give me a call if you like. You are angry with me, and rightly so. But we will have to talk about dismantling the house seeing as we are separating. We are an hour ahead right now, soon to be two, so don't call too late. I'll ring you again tomorrow." He forced himself to squeeze out, "Love you." He did not mention the train. He was not ready to be stopped just yet even though he knew he would have to face the inevitable. Even if he changed his name, he knew eventually he would be found. It was better to make it easy, as if he wasn't running away, but not just yet. His priority was to see his children. The call, however, was necessary.

The steward announced dinner. Quite a few new faces showed up in the dining car. Again, Oliver was seated with five different people, two who had begun their journey in Vancouver. They commiserated over the weather and lack of view. One fellow, Donald Montgomery, told jokes non-stop, and Oliver joined in at first, but as dinner wore on and drinks began to flow, Donald's stories became more and more risqué. Oliver was baffled at how unable Donald was to read the mood around him, how his filthy language and stories were causing others to leave in disgust. Finally, it was just Oliver and Donald at the table. Oliver let him blather away. Maybe he'd talk himself out and not bother anyone else again that evening. The danger was that he'd find Oliver a good listener and seek him out for more. He'd have to nip that in the bud.

"Donald, you're drunk, and I'm afraid I don't appreciate your filthy stories," he said as he got up.

Donald slurred his words trying to explain he was just kidding. He told Oliver in so many words that he didn't have a sense of humor.

"You're drunk, Donald. Good night." Let him think he was the prissy stick-up-the-ass Donald called him out to be as long as it kept him away. The steward quickly arrived to deal with the drunken man, and Oliver helped. They half carried Donald to his cabin two cars away, and Oliver left as security arrived and took over.

Chapter 10

How many times had Mona told him he did not have a sense of humor, this after she'd berated him publicly and privately? He had learned quickly to read her moods in order to protect himself and the children, a habit he practiced on everyone he met. No easy comradery, no light-hearted attachments. Judgmental? Perhaps. Definitely defensive.

When Frances watched the children before they were in school full days, Oliver, upon arriving home, would try to gauge what kind of evening they would have by the sort of music that was playing. While he took off his shoes, he listened for raised voices, sniffed the air for dinner cooking, and scanned the kitchen to see if the room was neat or a disaster. He hoped for quiet music—classical—Beethoven or Bach, no shouting or crying, and the smell of roasting meat and potatoes. If the kitchen was neat as well, he knew it was possibly a good day. If, however, no music played, just Mona screaming at her mother or the children, and the floor a minefield of dirty clothes, food wrappers and other refuse, he braced himself for the worst.

Often, he came home to silence. No one home. Mona may have been holed up in her bedroom, but he wouldn't open the door to find out. Let sleeping dogs lie. On such days, he felt a shift in the atmosphere of their old character home. How many decades had that house seen? How many different families had owned it and in later years rented it from the university? He doubted if the walls had been subjected to a family such as theirs, however. When he and Mona first moved in, he could feel the welcoming ambience of the place with its dark beams and polished hardwood floors. After they left, would the sensation of aggression, fear, and tension remain like scars etched on the walls and burned into the woodwork?

He loved the house with all its nooks and crannies, its built-in bookcases in every room but the bathrooms. Yes, it was in need of updating in places. The plumbing was unreliable as was the furnace, but at least they did not have to pay for those repairs. On days when he was alone in the house, he could almost relax. Frances was so good with the children. He'd watched her with Mona as well. She was expert at diverting Mona's outbursts, and often took the brunt, as did he, in order to protect Gavin and Gwendolyn. But when Frances brought the children home on one such quiet and empty-house day, she explained her need for having been out until he was there.

"She's having a bad day, Oliver. She tried to borrow money from me, but I don't have it to spare. Apparently, your account is overdrawn. She screamed at me, and when both kids started crying, she picked them up and tossed them in their beds. It was all I could do to keep her from them." This was as close to accusing her daughter of abuse as Frances would ever come.

"Frances, you have a bruise on your cheek. Did she hit you?"

"It's nothing. Don't worry about it. I'm used to her outbursts."

"Frances, we've got to do something. For the sake of the children, please support me in this. She's got to get help before she hurts them or you. God knows she's gone after me enough."

"I can't do it, Oliver. I may not be able to fix her, but I'm not going to help you lock her up. She can't help the way she is."

"For Christ's sake, Frances. I'm *trying* to help her. If you don't back me up, she will never get the help she needs. It will just be her word against mine, and you of all people, know how convincing she can be. Please, for her sake, let me call the police and have her committed for assessment at least."

Frances grabbed her coat and purse and headed for the door. "I can't do it, Oliver. I look into those eyes and see a terrified little girl, my little girl. I couldn't help her then and I can't stand by and watch her go through the horror of being put away. Don't ask me to do it. There's no real help in those places, anyway. I'll protect my grandchildren with my life, but I can't send my daughter to that hell."

"It's not like it used to be, Frances. She won't be put in a straitjacket. She'll be kept safe. So will the children. Think of them." He tried but it was no use. Frances walked away reassuring him that the children were being protected and that Mona said she wouldn't be home until late. He was grateful for that, at least. Frances apologized for not having dinner ready, but she was going out with friends that night and would be home late as well.

After making a supper of soup and sandwiches, Oliver bathed Gavin and Gwendolyn. He played Snakes and Ladders with them and read them a chapter of *Wind in the Willows*, Gavin's favorite book. He'd read it through at least half a dozen times, but every now and again, Gavin insisted upon revisiting it. Gwendolyn loved whatever her big brother loved. These were pleasant hours. He knew he could raise these beautiful children on his own much better than he could with Mona. They needed peace, routine, reliability, and he could give that to them. He tucked them in and gave each a kiss on the forehead.

"Goodnight," he began.

"Sleep tight," the two replied together from their separate rooms.

"Don't let the bedbugs bite," all three of them said before Oliver turned off the lights and closed their doors. He tried each knob to be sure the locks were secure.

This would be the last year Frances would have to mind them all day. First grade began for Gwendolyn in the fall, and Gavin would be in third grade. Oliver had enough seniority to have his schedule organized to match theirs, and Frances would have to watch them for only a few hours a day. The year after, maybe not at all. He was taking workshops in on-line teaching, with the intention of, as soon as possible, working from home. If he were honest, that was not his first choice. He'd choose for Mona to be normal. He'd choose to be able to teach his classes face-to-face. He liked teaching, liked his students. He'd choose to work without worry then come home to his wife and children and feel joy at being there. He would choose never to have a phone call like the one she made a few weeks later.

"You'd better get home and fast," Mona growled into the phone. "I'm going to kill all of them, my mother included. If you don't get here soon, I swear I will, and I'll record every bloody detail of it."

He stood his ground. Did not respond to Mona but hung up. He called Frances on her mobile, but she must have turned it off. He called their land line. Busy. He told himself he wasn't going to give in, not like he did the other times she threatened suicide. But not having contact with Frances did give him chills. After ringing Frances again without success, he called the police. Word for word, he told them what she was threatening to do. Mona kept the car at home insisting it was needed in case of an emergency with the children. He began walking, but fear for the children pushed him into a flat-out run.

The police were already there. Frances and Mona stood on the front porch talking to the officers as if nothing were wrong. When Oliver approached, all four of them turned to watch as he stepped onto the sidewalk and stood at the foot of the front steps. The look on their faces ground into him.

"You the one who called us?" a forty-something officer asked. He looked as if he was about to shove Oliver down the stairs he'd just climbed.

"Yes, my wife threatened to kill the children and herself. Her mother as well."

"You took your time getting here. You couldn't have been that worried."

"She's got the car. I had to run from my office. She's done this before. Threatened suicide, that is. I've raced home in the past to find her perfectly fine, just in need of some attention. This time I thought she was serious. I tried to call my mother-in-law, but she didn't answer her phone…"

Frances interrupted, "My phone is dead. I forgot to charge it."

The look on Frances' face told him she was lying. She likely couldn't get to the phone because she was dealing with Mona. He readied himself for what was coming, knew how he appeared. He looked to Frances for support, but she turned away and walked into the house. She would not back him up.

"Is that right, ma'am? Have you threatened suicide before?"

"No, of course not. I'm a mother with young children. I'd never do such a thing. He must have gotten it wrong. I called just to talk. The children were having a rough day. Their schedules are off, and there are two of them, so young and…" Mona looked around to see if Frances was near then added, "…and my mother is very demanding. I mean she's a help but she has to do things her way." Mona started to cry her big crocodile tears. The overwrought mother, the poor little woman. The officer reached as if to put a hand on her shoulder as she wiped the tears from her face. He stopped himself. Oliver recognized the urge to protect and defend her, had done it for years. No matter how hideous her behavior, he would fall for her vulnerability every time because sometimes it was real even if it wasn't this time.

Mona leaned toward the officer and, wiping her eyes, continued. "I'll be all right, thank you. I don't know why he does this. He overreacts sometimes. I'm sure he just got it wrong."

Oliver shook his head. "I'm telling you she called and said she'd kill the children and take a video of doing it. I'm not making this up. For Christ's sake, I'm a university professor. I'm not about to jeopardize my position on a whim. She made the threat." He thought of getting Brenda Macintyre involved. She had been a witness. But to do so would bring down the wrath of Mona upon her. Whatever Mona might do, it would be dangerous and it would make his workplace unthinkably difficult. Oliver backed down the stairs. The officer furthest from Mona followed him.

All was on record—his overreaction, her fear.

Oliver called his office, shaken, numb. He couldn't leave the children for his last class and got Brenda to monitor his students.

"They're writing an in-class essay. The topic sheets are printed and on my desk. There's nothing to do but monitor them as they write, and collect the papers."

"Of course, Oliver," Brenda said with concern. "I've got a lecture to prepare and this will force me to get it done. You deal with your family."

In this whole episode, his only consolation was that Frances had been with the children and they were safe. She might be overprotective of her daughter, but she would also protect Gwendolyn and Gavin. Oliver, moving like an automaton, walked to the back door and went into the house. He felt almost life-like but not quite connected, not quite human. He did not see Mona again that evening. She took off as soon as the police left, returning after everyone was in bed. "Thank God for small favors," Oliver whispered in the dark, listening as she walked through the house, grateful as she shut her bedroom door.

When Oliver walked through the door in the late afternoon the next day, all seemed calm. Frances had put dinner on. The house was clean and organized. He could hear the children playing in the basement rec room. The table was set, and Mona was curled up on the living room sofa reading.

"Where's Frances," he asked, looking from Mona to the children's rooms, not trusting the capricious calm.

"She's downstairs playing with the kids." Mona grinned at him. "Guess where I've been today?"

He was ready with a sarcastic response, but as usual, he kept it to himself. No need to stir up trouble any earlier than it would inevitably arise. "I am sure I haven't a clue. What were you up to?" Oliver stood in the archway between the living room and the kitchen, keeping an ear out for the children, ready to shield them from what Mona was winding up to deliver.

"Well," she began as she unfolded her legs and slowly stood to face him. "I've been to the police department. I had a lovely chat with an officer…let me see, what was his name?" She tapped her finger on her chin as she pretended to reach for the man's name. "Oh yes, Officer Frasier, Richard. He was one of the officers who came to my rescue yesterday after your silly outburst." Mona laughed. She turned away from him and walked toward the window. "Yes, he was very helpful. I asked him how to go about getting a restraining order. Against you. He was quite knowledgeable on the subject. Mind you, I didn't go through with it, the restraining order, that is. I just needed to drop a little hint, to reinforce my position. Just some added security." She dragged her hand along the back of the sofa as she walked behind it, putting a little more distance between them.

A whirlwind of emotions churned inside him, but he remained motionless. He did not approach her, nor did he back away.

"Is eliminating me from the picture something you could handle, Mona? I mean, could you manage the children on your own?" They both knew the answer. "You'd have to go back to work since half my income would certainly not be enough to support you." He held his tongue against adding *in the manner to which you have become accustomed*, keeping it as his private and sad little jab.

"Oh, no. Not at all. I simply solidified the impression the police department has of you should you ever decide to call them again."

"You're the perfect little victim, aren't you?" he did say out loud as she fluttered her eyelashes at him and smiled.

As always, no one but Oliver heard her.

Frances passed away from heart complications when the children were seven and nine. Although she wasn't babysitting anymore, they'd grown up with their grandmother and were greatly upset at the news, but it was Mona who took center stage, as usual, leaving them little opportunity to express their grief fully. At the funeral, Mona's display was embarrassing to all of them. She wore solid black including a thick veil over a hat that Oliver had never seen before. Black gloves, black shoes and hose, a long black skirt and a tight-fitting black jacket. She looked like something out of the eighteenth century. Oliver was grateful his mother-in-law's wish was to be cremated. He could picture Mona throwing herself on her mother's coffin had there been one. She would, in her dramatization of the lamenting daughter, likely have jumped into the grave if one had been dug. As it was, her loud wailing throughout the service directed stares their way.

Gavin and Gwendolyn sat on either side of Oliver, each hugging an arm, each trying to hide their tear-covered faces behind him. Mona's sister and brother attended but sat on the other side of the room. As soon as the service was over, and after talking to a few of Frances' friends, both fled the building without a word to Mona, Oliver, or the children. He understood their reluctance and wished for all the world he could flee with the pair to a distant world, one without Mona.

When they returned home after the service, Mona went straight to her room, took off her mourning clothes and came out into the living room in a pair of florid-red pants and a vibrant blouse. She poured herself a glass of wine and plunked down on the couch.

"Thank god that's over with," she said as if the effort of attending her mother's funeral was an annoyance that interfered with the important business of her day. At first, she did not respond to the shocked looks her children gave her.

"What are you looking at?" she hissed when she finally acknowledged them. "Did you expect me to wear black forever?"

The children fled to Oliver. He took them to the kitchen and started on dinner, something simple was all he could manage—salad and hamburgers. As he cooked, the children set the table. When called to eat, Mona took her plate of food to her room and ate alone.

Too upset to eat, the pair stared at their plates. Looking from one to the other, Oliver said, "Let's each tell about one special time we had with Grandma Frances. Just one," he said, "one each."

Gavin started first. "She took us out for milkshakes and told us not to tell anyone. It was our secret."

Gwendolyn laughed in agreement. She covered her mouth as if the secret were still to be kept. "She walked slow so we could look at things on the way to the park. She always saved the stuff I picked up for her. She called them her treasures."

Gavin nodded.

Oliver added, "I remember the great roast beef dinners she cooked. She made the best gravy in the world."

"Your gravy is good, Dad," Gwendolyn said.

"Your grandmother taught me how to make it, that's why."

One remembrance led to another, as Oliver knew it would, and between stories, the children ate. They each laughed and cried over Frances and felt better for the memories of her, all but Mona, concealed in her room, who seemed to have forgotten her mother had ever existed.

They had brought home flowers from the service, and after dinner, Oliver made smaller bouquets of white and pink roses for each of the children to keep in their rooms. He put a beautiful arrangement of white lilies and other pastel flowers on the table, but the next day, it was gone. He saw it in the garbage can when he took out the trash after dinner. She'd thrown it there. Out of guilt, he wondered? More likely she simply got rid of that which reminded her of Frances and the wicked way she had treated her. Mona never mentioned her mother again in sorrow or in joy.

Still distressed over her grandmother's death, a few days later Gwendolyn asked Oliver, "Isn't Mama sad that her mother died?"

"I am sure she is, in her own way. Everybody acts differently when in grief," he said. But there was different and there was Mona. "Perhaps she is in her room right now thinking about Grandma and going over all of her memories."

"She was a good grandma," Gwendolyn said, "so Mama must have a lot of good memories."

Oliver wished that were so. Perhaps there were, but he was not aware of even one. Mona did not speak much of her past, even of her father's early death. Frances had filled him in. But he sincerely hoped there were a few good memories. Unlike the memories his own little girl would carry with her for the rest of her life—the tantrums, the physical and verbal assaults. Not to mention the impossibility of living up to Mona's demands.

Oliver picked up Gwendolyn from a friend's house the following Saturday afternoon. The girls were skipping in Anna's driveway, and as they skipped, they sang:

On a mountain stands a lady
Who she is I do not know.
All she wants is gold and silver.
All she wants I dare not know.
So come in my partner, my partner, my partner,
So come in my partner, and dance along with me.

"Where do they learn these things," he asked Anna's dad who came out to greet him.

"They're born knowing them. They've got a few dozen of them."

"There was just me and my brother Derek," Oliver said. "We had no clue about skipping songs." He turned to Gwen when the girls stopped skipping to catch their breath. "Come on, Gwen. Time to go home." Gwen hugged him and said goodbye to Anna and her father. She skipped home down the street.

That evening was one of those rare occasions when Mona joined them at the table for dinner. Oliver brought up Gwendolyn's skipping and the song the girls sang, asked Gwen to sing it for her mother.

"My sister and I had a million of them. We were pretty good, too. Can you skip double Dutch?" she said to Gwen who shook her head.

"After supper, I'll teach you. We need two skipping ropes."

"I've got two," Gwen said, excited at the prospect of her mother skipping rope with her.

At moments like this, Oliver's hope rose, but so did his apprehension for which he chided himself not to be so negative. Perhaps this would be the breakthrough.

"I'll do the dishes. You two go and skip your hearts out. I want to hear lots of singing." He watched as Mona tied one end of each skipping rope to the fence. She showed Gwen how to turn the ropes first the one on the right then the left rope swinging inward. Gwen got the hang of turning. Her little face lit up as her mother jumped into the churning ropes and skipped.

Early in the morning just past eight o'clock,
You can hear the postman when he knocks.
Up jumps Gwendolyn to open the door.
One letter, two letters, three letters, four.

"Now keep counting as I skip—*five letters, six letters, seven letters…*" Mona reached thirty-one letters before she stopped the ropes. "Now your turn. Don't be afraid. Keep your eye on one rope, the one closest to you and jump in after it hits the ground. You have to duck a little to get under the second rope as it comes around."

Gwendolyn tried to jump into the turning ropes, but she kept getting tangled.

"Try again, Gwen. Don't be a baby. Don't be a quitter. Keep trying." Mona's voice was becoming shriller and louder the more frustrated she became with Gwendolyn.

"Ow," Gwen cried. "The rope hurts."

Oliver walked out to watch and to protect Gwendolyn if needed.

"Stop crying, Gwen. Get in there and jump. For once in your life, just try." Mona was shouting now.

Again and again, Gwendolyn tried, the plastic rope whipping her arms and legs.

"I can't do it, Mama. I'm trying, but I can't do it. Let's just play with one rope."

"For God's sake, Gwendolyn. Are you going to be a baby all your life? You're just like him," Mona snarled, pointing to Oliver. "Get a little gumption, will you? Where is your initiative? Just keep trying. It's not that hard, you sniveling little twit."

"That's enough, Mona." Oliver stepped in and yanked the ropes from her hands. "You've said more than enough. All she needs is a little practice and some patience from you. You can give her that, can't you?"

"Oh, yes. Big daddy come to save the day. What a hero. What a big dumb hero you are. No wonder these two are such namby-pamby wusses. Big hero daddy always coming to the rescue. To hell with that. Go to hell, the lot of you. Who needs you? I don't. I can stand on my own two feet, unlike little baby Gwen, here. I could skip double Dutch by the time I was ten." Mona looked with disgust at Oliver then Gwen.

"She's seven, Mona."

Mona was taken aback. For just a split second, she looked at Gwen as if recognizing her for the first time, then shook off her astonishment, turned on her heel, and fled into the house.

"Don't worry, Gwen. You'll get it when you practice with Anna. The two of you can learn it together. Mama's tired, that's all. Tired and sick. Remember what we talked about? When Mama acts like this, she is not really angry with you, she's angry with herself because she doesn't have the power to make things the way she insists they should be."

"She wants me to be perfect, but I'm not," Gwen sobbed.

"Nobody is. Not me, not Gavin, not anybody. Healthy people know this, but your mother is not healthy. She has some personality problems that she should get help for, but she just can't bring herself to get the help she needs. You need to take this to heart, my sweet, that you are just fine the way you are. Whether or not you can skip double scotch, or whatever it's called."

"Double Dutch, Daddy. All the big girls at school can do it."

"Okay, double Dutch. Whether or not you can do it won't make one tiny bit of difference in your life later on, and it doesn't make any difference to me. I love you just as you are, now go see if Anna is finished dinner and do some more skipping. Be home when the streetlights come on."

Gwen ran off. Gavin asked if he could go to his friend's, too, and off he went. Before he got beyond the driveway, Mona, dressed to kill, ran down the front sidewalk and jumped into a cab that pulled up to the curb and barely had time to stop. Off she went. Oliver was left alone to vent his rage on the soil of a new garden bed. *All she wants is gold and silver, all she wants I dare not know* ran through his mind as he sliced the earth with a spade, lifted a huge clod and stabbed it over and over again with the sharp edge.

Chapter 11

It was after ten when, showered and robed, Oliver stepped into the courtesy car. He hoped Donald wasn't there, didn't want another confrontation, but the only one present was Shirley seated at their table.

"Day two. So far so good?" she asked.

"I hope there's less rocking tonight," Oliver said. He sat down with his coffee, not spilling it this time.

"There will be. We're nearing the Prairies. We'll stop at Edmonton at about eleven. There'll be time to go out and take a walk." She looked him up and down, "But not dressed like that." They both laughed. Shirley, too, was dressed for bed. "It'll be smooth sailing now," she said as she split her pile of shortbread cookies with him.

"Is there a chessboard? Would you like a game?" he asked.

"There probably is. They have everything else, but I'm not much of a player. I can move the pieces, but I can't seem to strategize. I'm sort of a one-day-at-a-time kind of person. I don't really plan that much ahead. I like to take things as they come. It wouldn't be much fun for you or me. Any other game you'd like?"

Oliver thought about the games he'd played with Gwen and Gavin—kids' games. He liked the word games he had played with them as they got older. "Scrabble?" he offered.

Shirley went to the game cupboard and found a well-used box. "Hope all the letters are here." She opened the board and hefted the bag of wooden squares. "Seems pretty full. You draw first."

Oliver drew a letter then it was Shirley's turn.

"I got A," she announced. Oliver opened his hand. He'd drawn M and gave an involuntary shudder.

"They say when you shiver like that it means someone has walked over your grave," Shirley said as they threw their letters back in and drew seven others out.

"I've heard that, too," was all he could manage.

"So, what will you do in Toronto once you settle there," Shirley asked as they set up their letters on the holders.

"Oh, I'm not sure. Write, maybe. I've spent my life reading and analyzing literature. I could likely write a story or two."

"What would you write, romance, adventure, memoir, mystery?" Shirley spelled the word O-B-V-I-O-U-S. "That's sixteen and with the double letter score for the V and double-word score. Plus fifty for playing all my letters. That makes eighty-two. Woohoo!" Shirley shouted.

Oliver fiddled with his letters then sat back in his seat. "I'd write something to do with human nature. Try to figure out why a person does what he or she does, what makes them tick."

"That's a big task. You'll have to study psychology for that, I would guess. See what the experts have to say. Are you acquainted with any psychologists whose brain you can pick? What do you have?" Shirley insisted, peering at Oliver's tiles.

"Nothing. Nothing at all." Oliver stood up. "I'm sorry, Shirley. I'm not feeling well." He heard Shirley as he walked out of the car.

"Too bad," she said. "You've got a great word here. Worth lots of points," she called after him. But he did not turn back.

Hewitt. Would that man forever be thrown in his face? If psychologists had all the answers, why hadn't he done something to help Mona? That was easy enough. He must have liked Mona so needy, so dependent, always running to him. But she'd threatened suicide so often that he was surely running the risk of losing his plaything. Of course, Oliver was always there to rescue her, keep her from harm. Keep her for Hewitt. Oliver was likely just a pawn in his and her appalling game.

In his berth with the curtains drawn, Oliver shook with anger and fear. How many times had she threatened to hang herself? How many times had he talked her down, taken the noose from her neck, once even lifting her and slipping off the rope after she'd stepped off a chest in front of him? As always, never any witnesses. Never enough to have her committed on his word alone.

The train rocked gently. Oliver took an Ativan. His doctor prescribed him a few from time to time considering what he had to deal with. He'd rarely taken one when the children were home since he had to be alert for Mona's nocturnal rages. He'd taken more since Gwen left for university. Now that she was just about to receive her doctorate, and Mona was out of their lives, after this trip he hoped he would never have to take one again. He put in his earbuds and played a soundtrack of relaxing music he had selected some days ago. The piece he listened to fit his mood so precisely he had to look at the title— *Nothing Left to Lose*. How could this night be filled with so many coincidences? So many connections? So much of what he needed to leave behind? He would have wept had he not been so broken.

The next morning, they stopped in Saskatoon. The sun shone, and many of the passengers, including Oliver, left the train to stretch their legs and breathe the fresh brisk air. As with most of the stations they encountered, this one was in the middle of nowhere, but it felt good to get out and walk. The sky was intensely blue, and the clouds added depth and perspective stretching to infinity. Oliver was grateful for the cool air. He forced himself to take out his phone and make the dreaded call home, terrified she would answer, impossible as it was. Once again, he spoke to the answering machine, talking about the weather, the scenery although not mentioning where he was or that he was on the train from Vancouver to Toronto. He reinforced their impending divorce, making himself add *love you* to the recorded message once again. He couldn't say those words to Mona's face, but since she could not mock him or deflect his words, he could say them. Now, however, they were being said to the memory, not the fact of her. They were being said to help avoid blame from others. He would hold himself forever culpable.

Shirley stood beside him as he clicked off his phone. "You do have someone back home."

What was he to do? He felt he could trust Shirley, but his cautiousness would not let him reveal more than necessary. He said, "Yes, I do. My wife. We're estranged."

"Estranged? What an old-fashioned word. Do you mean you're separated?"

"Yes, I guess we are though not legally. We haven't been getting along for some time now. She left. I've left. Nothing more to it. No going back, is more like it."

"Sorry to hear that, Oliver. It's sad when that happens."

Oliver nodded as if he agreed with her and after answering that he was feeling much better, thank you, walked away.

Twenty-five minutes later, they were back on the train and swaying toward their destinations. Shortly after the train reached full speed, Shirley stood over him. "Come with me to the observation car."

He looked up from his book and shook his head. "I can see just fine from here," he said, turning his face toward the large side window.

"You won't regret it. I promise."

Oliver sighed. He'd been rude to her last night, feigning illness and running off as he had from their game of Scrabble. He couldn't refuse her again. Closing his book, he dutifully followed her to the glass-domed car.

"Have you ever seen such immensity?" she asked as she looked at the vast fields of wheat—some harvested, others waiting—stretching to eternity on both sides of the train.

Oliver had read that many people experienced agoraphobia when faced with the Prairies for the first time. Now he understood why. He was city born and bred. Nothing, not even looking out across the ocean, had prepared him for this span of land and sky, for the unencumbered view. No boundaries to push against. No limitations to confine or restrict. The ocean reflected light, let it bounce off sparkling waves, but the earth absorbed it and performed the alchemy of turning something base into fields of gold. They were traveling through the Prairies on a fast-moving train, but he could imagine the impact it must have had on early settlers standing in the middle of this flat expanse or attempting to cross it by horse and wagon. What stuff the pioneers were made of to challenge this powerful landscape. What would Oliver have done with such freedom?

Everyone around him vanished. Oliver's thoughts focused on the great space before him. Time stood still, and the power of the land filled him. He didn't recognize such power, mistook it for anger. And he was angry, angry with himself for getting caught in the quicksand of his miserable life. Angry with Mona who had deceived him, used him, battered him down to nothing. He felt rage at the thought of Hewitt, a monster himself, Mona's lover. He had used her as she had used Oliver—a chain of misery and horror. Rage at the memory of Gavin, just fourteen, threatening to tell the school counselor about her abuse and Gwendolyn joining him.

Chapter 12

Mona looked at the three of them standing together, a force against her. Her grin turned ugly as she chuckled.

"And what are you going to tell the counselor? That your mom beats your dad? That you have decided to live with your dad and leave your own mother? Well, guess what? He's not who you think he is." She stared into Gavin's face as she spoke, pointing at Oliver. "He's not your father. He's just a cuckold. Do you know what a cuckold is, my dear son?"

"Shut up, Mona. Stop it. He's just a child. This is nothing for a child to hear. Think of him. Think of them both." Oliver pleaded with her, vainly trying to reach some part of her that harbored a molecule of empathy for someone other than herself.

Ignoring him she continued ever louder as Oliver pulled both children to himself and tried to protect them from words that tore through their minds and hearts. "A cuckold is a man who is so inadequate that his wife has sex with another man. It's a word that comes from the cuckoo bird who lays its eggs in another bird's nest so it doesn't have to raise its own young. You're going to tell your counselor that you want to live with your father? Well, that's fine, but you will have to go live with my good friend Hewitt. He is your father, not this, this..." She dismissed Oliver with a wave of her hand.

Oliver grabbed her arm, pulling her off balance, as he and the children dashed past her, out the door and into the car. They drove to Jericho Beach, Gwendolyn sobbing as they went. Once there, facing the ocean, they sat in the car, Oliver stunned at the depths of cruelty Mona had reached. Gavin's eyes were red with tears and as a result of the angry swipes he made across his face to hide them. Gwendolyn gasped for breath through her tears. In elongated and sob-broken syllables, she cried, "Daddy."

Oliver knew. Somewhere deep within him the truth sat like a viper ready to strike. They were not his offspring. But he was their father. In every other way, he was their father. As Gavin grew taller, he shared the same build and coloring as Hewitt. Gwendolyn, too, was blonde and willowy, but he'd told himself except for her fair hair, she took after her mother. Neither child had Oliver's stocky build or dark hair. He'd just never put what he knew into words. Mona had done that for him.

He should have done something to prepare them for this hideous moment, hinted at it or fed them a few details a little at a time. But how does a man go about telling his children he is not their father? And now that they knew, what would happen? They might hate him for keeping that fact from them. They might choose to get to know Hewitt, and he would have to let them. It was their right. But how could he prepare them for the kind of man Hewitt was? Or for the kind of hurt they would face when he rejected them as he certainly would. As Oliver hoped he would. He was being self-centered. But sharing his children with Hewitt? It was enough that he had shared his wife, unwillingly and initially unwittingly. It was enough that he was forced to share their lives with Mona.

Calm was a long time coming as they sat in the car and looked out across the water. Aside from Gwendolyn's cries, the first to speak was Gavin. "Is it true? Is Hewitt our father?" He almost whispered the words as if saying them too loudly would make a horrible idea come true. His fists clenched as he spoke.

Oliver turned to him and with righteous strength said, "He may be your biological father, but I am the one who loves you more than any other person on this earth could love you."

Gavin threw himself into Oliver's arms and Gwendolyn nearly leaped over the seat to grasp Oliver with all of her young might. He assured them he wasn't going to leave them, that he would be with them as long as they needed him.

"I'm not going to live with him," Gavin said and Gwendolyn reaffirmed.

"I know," was all Oliver could say. He could not promise them that would never happen. He was helpless in what he could say and much more in what action he could take. He could only react to whatever Mona decided to do.

"Why can't you, me, and Gwen just leave? You could get a job at another university," Gavin pleaded.

How could Oliver explain a court system that was not always on the side of justice or a child-welfare system that seemed to exist to justify itself? He tried, however, and explained to them what lawyers had told him, that he had no power to do what was certainly in their best interest. But children believe that fathers cannot be powerless. They remained confused, and Oliver prayed they would not hate him for it.

When their tears were spent and all sobs subsided, they walked along the beach, Gwendolyn's hand in his and, from time to time, Gavin's hand in hers. As the sun began to set, Oliver suggested a supper of hotdogs and fries at a kiosk. They sat on a huge log and ate, watching the tide come in and the stars break through the evening sky. Until Oliver's phone rang.

"You're going to leave me now, go ahead," Mona began without giving him a chance to say hello. "Go ahead. I'll take the children and live with Hewitt. You don't have a chance in the world of having them with you, so go ahead. Leave." She hung up without Oliver saying a word.

He knew she was right just like he knew he would never leave them. From that moment on, it was anger that kept him going, anger contained enough not to destroy her but enough to give him the strength to trudge forward waiting for his day of freedom.

His anger was not contained the following week, however, when Hewitt showed up at Gavin's championship soccer game. He had the nerve to sit on the edge of the bleacher by Oliver and ask how Gavin's team was doing.

"What the hell are you doing here," Oliver said, not concerned about who heard him.

"Why shouldn't I be here?" Hewitt leaned forward looking out at the field, at Gavin. "I was quite a soccer player in my day," he added. "How about you? Play much?" Hewitt laughed. Oliver shoved him off the bleachers. He jumped down and punched Hewitt in the head as the man got up from the ground. Hewitt was taller and athletic, and Oliver knew he didn't have a chance against him, but that did not matter. What mattered was that his rage was spent on the man who was a threat to his children. *His* children. The children he had raised, protected, and loved. Oliver got in one more good punch hitting Hewitt's chest, knocking the wind out of him. Hewitt stumbled back and was about recovered enough to finish Oliver when several men from the field and bleachers stepped in to break up the fight.

"That's enough. This is a kid's game," said one angry woman.

Two men pulled Hewitt and Oliver apart. "Knock it off, you two. Some example you are," this from the man who held back Oliver. It was over before it had gone too far. Oliver dropped his arm, and Hewitt shrugged off the hands that held him.

Hewitt called back as he left, "You'll pay for this, Eastmund. You wait. You'll pay."

Oliver, triumphant that he'd at least got in a few good hits, put his arm around Gavin who'd pushed through the crowd to get to him. "It's all right. It's over. Go back to your game. I'm okay. Everything's okay now." He took his hanky and wiped the sweat from his face and saw his bloodied knuckles. He looked at Gavin and shrugged. Gavin, who had been behind the adults and could not have seen much of the fight, gave him a worried smile and an unexpected hug and went with his coach back to the game. Oliver wondered what cost Hewitt would exact from him. Before sitting back in the bleachers, he apologized to those who had intervened and looked around for Gwendolyn. She was enjoying time with her friends in the nearby playground, unaware of what had taken place. They were fine, at least for now. And now was all they had.

Chapter 13

"Relax, partner," Shirley said as she patted his arm. He'd hit the padded seat beside him with his fist and sat with hands clenched.

Surprised that he had acted out his fight with Hewitt, Oliver apologized. "I'm sorry," he said. "Something about this landscape makes me feel anger like I haven't felt for a long time."

"It's powerful, that's for sure. Anger and power seem to go hand in hand, but there are other kinds of power as well. Don't forget that. Not all power is born from anger." Shirley said this as she looked straight into his face.

Oliver looked back at her as he gained control over his rapid breath. He took a few deep ones and blinked once then twice. A small smile, a weary one, a little sheepish, played on his lips and he looked away. "How'd you get so wise?" he asked.

"That's a long story, a life story," Shirley said. "Too long to tell on this trip. We'd have to go back and forth across the country for me to tell the whole thing."

"I hear what you are saying," Oliver said. "I certainly hear you."

They sat in silence, Oliver gathering a different kind of strength from the land and Shirley simply taking in the vista. "It's almost lunch time," Shirley said. "You stay here. I'm going to talk to the steward. I'll be right back."

Oliver wondered what she was planning, but he was resolved to stay in this car with this view. He was hungry, starving, but not for food. All the other passengers made their way to the dining car, and he was glad to be left alone. When Shirley got back, she grinned and told him that lunch was all set. In a few minutes, a porter brought in a table and attached it to a hinge on the wall. Another set the table with linen and cutlery, and a third, the steward himself, rolled in a cart with lunch for two that he deftly set on the table.

"You did me a favor yesterday by calling out that obnoxious dinner guest, so I'm returning the favor. We don't normally serve lunch in the observation car, but this is a special case." With that, the steward bowed slightly and left.

They remained in the observation car long after lunch was cleared, right up until dinner time. Even then, Oliver refused to leave. Shirley left him alone with his thoughts and with a sunset that held out promise and hope even if he had images of ghost riders chasing the devil's herd across the never-ending sky. Power. Power and beauty, real beauty. Nature's beauty, true and honest, a gift without strings. The light softened with the evening clouds floating in from the west and with the twilight, that mid-blue, the half-light that pulled at his heart and evoked a yearning so strong if he were standing it would bring him to his knees. It was the color of love. Not the red garish love of Valentines or romance, but something bigger, more powerful. A universal love, an archetypal power that surpassed all.

When the train reached Winnipeg, it was almost nine o'clock in the evening. They would stop here for two hours, so Oliver disembarked and searched through the huge station and the surrounding city. He bought himself dinner from a food truck. Again, he made a phone call with his prepared message for the answering machine. This time, he stopped before saying *I love you.*

He did not go to the courtesy car that night after showering and changing but decided to call Gwendolyn and Gavin from his berth instead and report on his progress. They were happy to hear from him, and Theresa got on the phone with Gavin. She insisted that Oliver stay with them as long as he liked.

"We've renovated the coach house for you, Dad," she said even though he could hear Gavin in the background telling her to shush and not spoil the surprise. "You can live here forever, if you like," she said and she sounded like she meant every word. "You're going to be a grandfather soon," Theresa added, letting all the surprises tumble out at once. She apologized that she couldn't wait until he got there to tell him.

"When? How long?" Oliver said, his heart racing with joy.

"In about four months," Gavin said excitedly. "We don't know if it's a boy or girl. We don't want to know. It's one surprise we are keeping." All three of them laughed.

"That's wonderful news. Great news. I'm so happy for you both, for all of us." Oliver, overwhelmed with emotion, held back his tears and cleared his throat a few times. He barely managed to contain himself. "I can't wait to see both of you. I'll be in Toronto at around nine thirty in the morning, day after tomorrow. I'll get a cab to your place."

"You will not," said Gavin. "We'll be there to meet you, the two of us and Gwen. She's so excited I'm surprised she hasn't driven out to meet you already. Why didn't you fly?"

How could he explain to Gavin without bringing up a lot of unpleasantness, without mentioning his mother? Gavin had no interest in hearing anything about Mona, that was clear enough. "I needed time, Gav. I needed some time to get a feel for my new-found freedom. I've told you I'm not going back for anything except to pack up the house, so I had some thinking and planning to do, a few loose ends to tie up in my own mind, at least." He could not explain to Gavin that initially he had been afraid of this new freedom, afraid that it would be snatched away, afraid of what the shock of it coming upon him suddenly might do to him. Ridiculous fears, but fears just the same, and he needed time to sort them out. Just a little time to acclimatize to his new life. But as expected, Mona interfered with his simple tactic to leave her, divorce, move on. And now, he needed time to be sure, to be very sure, that he would not be blamed for her last performance even if he carried that blame forever in his heart.

"Let's not get into that now. She has no idea where you are, where we are, so she can't contact us." Oliver changed the subject. "By the way, did you get the paperwork ready for my name change?" It was no longer necessary, but the name change would bring him closer to Gavin and Gwen in their shedding of the old and putting on of the new.

"Just waiting for your signature, Mr. Rook."

Oliver said, "Good man. I'll practice my best John Hancock."

When Theresa and Gavin met in his second year at university and were married shortly after graduation, Oliver was concerned, but his worrying had been groundless. Soon, Gavin was articling at a prestigious law firm making junior partner in record time. He was that good, and Theresa's family was that wealthy. Theresa's grandparents had left their Rosedale home to her parents who had given it to their daughter, their only child. Gavin and she were now expecting their first child. Oliver was grateful for his son's settled life. After all he had been through, Gavin deserved everything he had. He was a good son, a good man and would be an amazing father.

After the first thrill of discovering that he would be a grandfather and had a home to go to as well, Oliver felt more alone in his berth than he had since his journey began. If all went without a hitch, he would never feel lonely again. "Please let everything work out for once in my damned life," he whispered into the night. It was not a prayer, for he was beyond that now, had no right to pray for anything.

As he wavered between sleep and wakefulness, Oliver questioned again his decision to stay with Mona for the years after Gwendolyn left for university. He could have taken early retirement at sixty and spared himself the last few years of misery, but he was still paying off debts, her debts, and he needed a full pension, had to have it since there were no savings. As soon as every obligation had been paid off and he had put in enough time, he'd retired at the end of the summer term. He'd had his first pension check just before leaving and knew there were no glitches in that area. Just before he'd left, he addressed an envelope of money to Mona and left it on the kitchen table where he had always left her some cash. He also added a note saying that this money would have to last her the month. The utilities, which were in his name, would be disconnected at the end of the month. He also explained that he had given the university notice that they would be out of the house by then as well, so she'd better find herself another place to live. She should contact a lawyer, he also wrote, and he would meet with them when the time came. But now, all was subterfuge.

Freedom. Relief. Sorrow. Fear.

Chapter 14

Hewitt's threatening words hurled at Oliver after their brief fight wormed their way into his thoughts. "You'll pay for this," he'd threatened. But it wasn't Hewitt who'd made him pay, it was Mona. If you really want to hurt a man, he learned, hurt his children.

Every September, the university held a welcome-back get-together for the humanities division. They gathered in the garden of a quaint stone house surrounded by tall hedges with a small opening to a green space and a street behind the yard. Oliver, Mona and the children attended as did the families of all of the division's instructors. To Oliver's disgust, Hewitt was there as well. He had the gall to approach them.

Holding a glass of wine, and smiling that insidious smile of his, Hewitt announced, "I've been offered a teaching position here in the psychology department. Lucky me. I guess we'll be seeing more of each other."

Oliver dumped his drink and said, "Not if I can help it." He shoved his empty glass into Mona's hand and walked away. Gavin and Gwendolyn went to join Oliver when Mona did her worst.

"You two," she said motioning to the children. "Stand over there with Hewitt. Let's get a picture of the three of you together."

"No," Gavin all but shouted over his shoulder at his mother. "I'm not standing near *him*." He continued walking away.

"You'll do as I say," Mona said loudly enough that other instructors, their families, and the dean turned to look.

Oliver paused in this retreat and came back toward them. Gwendolyn approached Hewitt in an attempt to appease her mother and take the attention away from Gavin.

"Get back here, NOW!" Mona cried. She ran up to Gavin and whispered loudly in his ear, loud enough for Gwendolyn, Oliver and Hewitt to hear but no one else, "Do you want me to announce to this crowd that Hewitt is your real father? I'll do it. Trust me, I will."

With an adolescent's scowl of disgust, fourteen-year-old Gavin said, "Yeah, tell the world what a slut you are while you're at it," and continued to walk away. He'd let go of his fear of her.

Mona caught up to him behind the tall hedge that hid the crowd in the garden of the meeting house. She slapped him hard across the face then swung with a backhand catching him on his other cheek. Gavin was shocked but just for a second. He lifted a fist and was about to strike back when Oliver stepped between them.

"Get away from him, Mona. Touch him again, and I'll live up to your accusations."

Two couples from the gathering wandered past the hedge. Mona looked their way. Oliver put his arm around Gavin and quickly led him off toward the car. Gwendolyn, looking sick and disheveled, joined them saying, "I threw up on his shoes. She made me stand by him, but I got sick."

Oliver put his arm around her as well and held her to his chest. He said, "Good for you. It's all right. You're going to be okay."

Hewitt came at a fast trot from the garden. As he stopped to shake off his shoe, his look of repulsion was directed toward Gwen, but Oliver blocked her view as he helped her into the car. Hewitt fled in the opposite direction. Mona, left standing alone, headed for the closest car, which was Oliver's. He was tempted to drive away and leave her behind, but the scene she would make with his colleagues was something with which he couldn't deal. She got in and immediately began screaming. Oliver, a prisoner in the car, remained stoically silent as did Gavin and Gwen.

He was driving away from the rose-covered meeting house toward their home when out of the blue, Mona, frustrated that no one was responding to her rants, lifted her legs and pummeled the windshield. Oliver reached over to stop her, but she continued slamming her heels into the glass until it cracked. In a move as sleek as a cat's, she lowered her feet and swung her fist with everything she had. Her punch hit the side of Oliver's head. He lost control of the car. Off the road it flew. They dropped through a shallow ditch, launched up the other side, and almost flipped. The children screamed. Mona was the only one not wearing a seatbelt. When the car smashed into a tree, she was thrown into the already crazed windshield. Oliver turned to the children. They were terrified but unhurt. He looked at the unconscious Mona and hoped for the worst, but she moaned and put her hand to her bloodied head.

In a second's searing thought, he understood in his bones how easy it would be to reach over and twist her head until her neck snapped. But the children were there. He would never inflict that trauma upon them. Neither would he extend his hand to kill another human being, no matter what, but having the knowledge that he could was some measure of consolation. That he had come to the place where he entertained such a thing, even for a moment, shocked him, so in a panicked reflex to mitigate such an idea, he said to himself, *Let it ever remain just a thought*.

The police, an ambulance, and a fire truck arrived at about the same time. The paramedics worked on Mona and the police took statements from Oliver and the children.

When the officer returned after checking Oliver's license, he said, "We've got quite a file on you."

"I'm sure you have, but you'd better listen this time. She needs help. She is mentally ill and needs treatment. I can't get her to go, but you can have her admitted under the mental health act. I've been trying to protect my children all these years—over fourteen years—but it is becoming impossible. You've got to help us, help her, but certainly help my children." Oliver took his hand away from the side of his face where Mona had struck him. The officer looked at him, at the welt that was growing by his temple, and wrote in his notebook.

"I'll see what we can do, sir," he said. Oliver felt he was finally heard. It helped that Gavin and Gwendolyn gave the same report as he had, and that they were old enough to be listened to. The paramedics checked the three of them over, but they came out of the crash physically unscathed. Mona was taken away by ambulance. The car was too damaged to drive.

They came home by taxi, and Oliver hugged both children as they sat out in the back garden. The yard, after his and the children's hard work, was a peaceful paradise. Summer vacations spent working on the flower and vegetable beds had resulted in this one refreshing place where they could unburden themselves after facing the daemon. Today, in particular, the three of them needed that peace which arrived only in Mona's absence.

When Gwendolyn went off to pick flowers for the table, Oliver turned to Gavin. "You've been through a lot today," he began lightly. "We all have."

"It was all my fault. The accident. If I didn't talk back to her, it wouldn't have happened," Gavin said, choking on his words, trying not to cry.

"No, son. It wasn't your fault. You are not responsible for how others behave. We're each responsible for what we say and do. You are not to blame."

Gavin said nothing. He was slouched back in his deck chair looking as miserable as he surely felt. Oliver had to talk to him. He had to make his son see that his actions today would determine the man he would become, but his fury over Mona's behavior threatened to allow him to give his son a pat on the back for taking a stand.

"Gavin," Oliver began as he looked out across the yard, "what kind of man do you want to grow up to be? What is it that makes a man good or even great?"

Gavin shuffled his feet beneath his chair. He looked down into the glass of water he held in both hands, and after a long time, he shrugged his shoulders and muttered, "I don't know."

Oliver tried again. "I saw you raise your fist to your mother today, and before you think I'm going to give you hell for that, I'm not. I just have to ask you something. How did that make you feel afterward?"

Gavin couldn't look at him. Again, he looked down and said nothing, but his shoulders began to shake. He put his glass on the table and brought both fists up to his eyes to stem the tears of shame and anger.

"You probably have the idea that I stepped in to protect your mother from you or to protect you from her. The truth is, son, I stepped in to protect you from yourself."

Gavin wiped his face hard and turned his head to look at Oliver, his eyes narrowed skeptically.

Oliver continued, watching Gwen who was building a bouquet of the last of the dahlias and sedum, too far away to hear their conversation. "Have you ever seen me strike your mother?"

Gavin said, "No," and sniffed loudly.

"Have you ever heard me threaten to hurt your mother?"

Gavin shook his head.

"One of the characteristics of a man is strength. But there are different kinds of strength, Gav. Of course, a man may be physically strong, usually stronger than a woman. That kind of strength allows a man to protect his family and others from physical harm."

Gavin sat up and looked at Oliver. "Like you did when you punched Hewitt?"

"Yes, that's true. I tried to protect you and your sister from being upset." But it was more than that. He had lofty words for Gavin, but what had he done himself but be the aggressor just to get even with Mona? He was being hypocritical, but something more was at stake here than his own regression. "Another kind of strength is knowing what is right and acting on it even when everything inside of you tells you to lose control and lash out. Even if society tells you it would be understandable if you lost control because of some injury to your dignity, your feelings, your heart tells you that it wouldn't be right, so you don't. You don't hit, you don't abuse in any way, physically or verbally. That's called moral strength, ethical strength. If you do cross the line and lose control, the one you lash out at will be hurt, but the guilt and shame that you feel afterward knowing you had become the kind of person who could lose control and who could hurt someone you love will last a lifetime."

Oliver paused for a few seconds to let his words sink in before beginning again. "If you cross the line once, it will be easier and easier to cross it again and again until you become a man who is as morally and ethically corrupt as any bully. Do you understand what I'm saying?"

Gavin put his face in his hands again and mumbled through his tears, "I called her a slut," and he sobbed.

Oliver let him cry it out for a few minutes. He knew the conflict raging in Gavin's young heart. His entire life had been spent trying to extract just a molecule of love and attention from his mother without success. Now this. He was teetering on the brink of severing ties with her, Oliver knew. He himself was perpetually perched on that fence with only the children keeping him from jumping to the other side. Gwen looked over at them with concern, but she stayed at the back of the garden.

"Something that will help you get back on track would be to apologize to your mother."

Gavin sat up and looked at him, shocked. "Me apologize to her? She's the one..."

"Yes, son. You're right. She is the one who caused all this pain, but it is you I am worried about. If you don't apologize, you will carry the shame and guilt around with you forever. You will think of it every time you look at her or she comes to mind. What you focus on you become. Is your plan to become a man filled with shame and anger, one who behaves shamefully and acts out that anger? Or do you hope to be a man who is comfortable with himself, a man who has done the right thing, the best thing, in spite of pain and suffering. What's your goal, to be a morally strong man or just a tough tyrant?"

Gavin said nothing. Eventually, he relaxed back into his chair. Gwen came up to them with her bouquet of flowers and announced she was going into the house to get a vase. When she left, Oliver added one more thing he had learned living with Mona.

"Do you think your mother feels as upset as you do about what you said to her?"

Gavin didn't respond right away, and Oliver gave him the space he needed to come to his own conclusion.

"She doesn't feel anything except mad most of the time. She doesn't care what anyone says. Does she even cry over all the stuff she's done?" He asked this looking at Oliver for a brief second, gauging his reaction.

"She cries. She doesn't want to be this way," Oliver said, but she couldn't get off the hook that easily. She had moments of clarity in which she could make other choices like the choice for therapy. Gavin was not going to bear any of the guilt for his mother's behavior, not if Oliver could help it. "It's just that she won't get the help she needs and that she could have in order to make changes. But that doesn't mean any of what she does is excusable or acceptable. It means you, Gwendolyn, and I are not to blame. We still have to act like good and decent people, no matter what goes through our minds or even what we feel." Oliver knew this was true, but how many times had he wished Mona gone or worse. He would not act on those thoughts, but that was not because he felt particularly honorable. It was more likely that he was a coward, and as she'd said, not a real man.

"I will never be as strong as you." Gavin paused, still not looking at Oliver but out beyond the yard and the fence, out toward the distant trees and the snow-tipped mountains. "But I'll try," he said, then looked at Oliver and nodded.

"Good man. Good man." In his heart, however, Oliver knew himself not to be a strong man, not a particularly good man. He often felt inadequate to the job of being a father. He should have left years ago, taken the children with him and fought it out. He could have quit his job and gone on welfare. He would have had legal aid then, court costs paid for. He could have fought for them. But they were not his, and he would lose. Hewitt had never claimed them, that was clear enough, and Mona would have tired of them, used them only as leverage to harass him. She would never give the children to him simply because, without reservation, more than he loved her, he loved them. And he did, desperately. As he watched Gavin help Gwendolyn fit the overabundance of flowers into a vase, his heart almost broke. He had to protect these two not from strangers or monsters under their beds but from their own mother and father. His poor children.

Nothing. The police did nothing. Mona, apparently, was a model patient while in hospital. When Oliver called a day later to see how she was, as soon as the nurse knew he was her husband, her tone changed. Very coldly she said to him, "Mrs. Eastmund will be fine. No scarring. We will keep her for a few days to watch for concussion. Call before you come to pick her up."

But he didn't call. Gavin made good on his word and called his mother to apologize and hung up very shortly afterward. He did not tell Oliver her response and Oliver didn't pry. Gavin went to his room and closed the door behind him without saying a word. He stayed there until bedtime when he came out to brush his teeth and get ready for bed, but he did not offer to share what the conversation with his mother had been.

Neither Oliver nor the children went to the hospital to see her, and she did not call them. The one small hope he had, that perhaps now she could be declared insane, was dashed. The insurance company refused to pay one cent more than the lowest bluebook amount after the accident no matter how hard Oliver fought. It wasn't enough to buy a new car, so they lost it.

He was still paying off their debts from the last fifteen years, so there was no hope of even a well-used car. Oliver could walk to work. They lived only a few blocks from the schools the children attended. They would all have to manage, including Mona.

Upon her release, she did not call Oliver. Instead, she must have called Hewitt, but he brought her right back home. Oliver watched them through the living room window as they sat in Hewitt's car in the driveway. In spite of her bandaged head, her mouth was twisted in rage, obviously screaming at him. Hewitt, cool as could be, got out of the car and tossed, onto the lawn, a paper bag filled with her belongings that likely he'd brought to the hospital. He went around to the passenger's side of the car, opened it, and pulled Mona out, pushed her along to the sidewalk. Oliver stepped onto the porch.

"She's all yours. I've been offered a tenure-track teaching position at Dalhousie," he said, grinning at him as if they were friends. "I'm off to Halifax." He waved at Oliver, got in his car and drove away. Mona shrieked after him.

When Hewitt was out of sight, Mona grabbed the tossed bag and stormed into the house. Oliver followed.

"Don't talk to me," she shouted at him. She held her hand up to his face and stomped by him, went to her room, and slammed the door.

So much for the peace Oliver, Gwen and Gavin had had for the past few days. What a sad state to be in, to be happier when his wife was in hospital than when she was at home. How had he become so callous? Oliver doubted he would ever again be a truly compassionate human being, at least where it concerned Mona. But for the children's sake, like Gavin he would try.

Chapter 15

The train rocked Oliver to sleep, but he took with him into his dreams the terrible self-recrimination that he had not been able to completely protect his children. *His* children. He'd raised them and loved them more than his own life. That his wife and Hewitt had fucked like dogs in the street didn't make them parents. Hewitt abandoned Gavin and Gwendolyn and, for that matter, Mona in the end. Hewitt used her until she came with too many complications.

Oliver hovered between sleep and wakefulness, aware of every little town at which the train stopped. Elma at eleven thirty-five, Rice Lake at twelve twenty-two, Canyon at two twenty-one. He got up and dressed just before Sioux Lookout. At five A.M., he stepped off the train into the predawn light. Stars still flickered, and a fingernail moon held its place in the transitional blue of the sky. Change. He was on the verge of change, and his fear was that it would likely be snatched away. *But what could happen*, he reasoned with himself. He'd done nothing. She had been kept in the dark about where Gavin and Gwen lived all the years they went to university. She didn't even know their last name, so she could not have told Hewitt, not that he would come after them to claim them now. It was hard letting the fetters drop. He was free, but he was dragging his chains with him because they had kept him company for so many years. They were familiar. And they were fashioned from guilt.

He breathed in the cold autumn air. There was not much to see at the station or in its surroundings. Oliver looked at the train and felt a wave of revulsion. The bleak beige and gray interior of that beast no longer held its initial appeal. Talking about the trivialities of life with more strangers was exhausting. Tired of being polite and affable, he wished he could take his breakfast to an empty car and not be in contact with anyone. But at this point, that train was the only way to his children and a chance at a life of freedom, if that life was his to grasp.

As at the other stations before Sioux Lookout, enormous hanging baskets of flowers as well as several large pots decorated the outside of the station. All were filled to overflowing. It was a wonder to him that they survived the cold nights, but being above ground level most likely helped. Would these beautiful arrays of vivid colors and perfectly-shaped plants be at every station, reminding him of the garden he had worked so hard to construct and maintain? He turned from the vision of what it once was, what it had become.

The train left Sioux Lookout at quarter to six and swayed hypnotically along the tracks. They passed station signs so quickly he couldn't read them. At eight thirty, breakfast was called, and he was pleased to be seated with Shirley and another woman, very elderly and hard of hearing. The steward announced her as Mrs. Hartford. She smiled as Shirley and Oliver spoke to her, but she couldn't hear a thing and was not eager to engage in conversation. It was just as well since Oliver and Shirley didn't speak much even to each other. The dining car was about half full because many passengers got off at the Sioux Lookout stop, and others likely had had breakfast before boarding.

"I didn't thank you for lunch in the observation car yesterday. It was very kind of you to arrange it," he said.

"Well, you looked like a man who was getting a little stir crazy after being cooped up for so long. Besides, I love looking out at the Prairies. Makes me feel generous." Shirley smiled at him, and he laughed a little.

"No one ever starved on this train," Oliver said after several minutes of silence. "I've eaten more in the last couple of days than I'd eat in a week at home. I may skip lunch today and walk through the train to get some exercise. You're right. I am getting a little cabin fever."

"Just be careful where you end up on your walk. We may lose a car or two at Hornepayne. We stop there if anybody is waiting for the train or if there are goods to be picked up or dropped off. You don't want to be left behind."

"I'll bear that in mind. Thanks for the heads up."

"You coming to the courtesy car tonight so we can finish that Scrabble game?" she asked.

He'd been rude to Shirley, walking out on their game as he had. And she'd been witness to his rising anger in the observation car. He owed it to her to be civil and said light heartedly, "Sure, why not."

After breakfast, Oliver found the steward. "I won't be having lunch in the dining car today," he said.

The steward asked with concern, "Nothing is wrong, is it, sir?"

"Just the opposite, thank you. You feed us too well. I've got to get some exercise. I'll be back for dinner."

The steward chuckled as Oliver jogged in place for just a few seconds. He walked the length of the train as far as he was allowed to go and back to his seat again. Three times he did this, and then he stopped at a snack bar to pick up a sandwich and coffee, a small lunch compared to the elaborate servings in the dining car.

At three thirty, they reached Hornepayne. He got off the train for some fresh air and to make a call to Vancouver. He had to make his voice sound desperate at this point or simply resigned that Mona would not answer his calls.

"Mona, would you please just answer the phone?" He began after much beeping of the answering machine. "At least, call me back. We can be civil about this divorce. I'm afraid if you don't get in touch with me, I'm going to have to call Mrs. White next door to check up on you, and I know how you feel about her. Text me rather than talk, if you like, just so I know nothing's wrong. Bye for now. I'll call again unless you call or text me." He hoped he sounded concerned and not guilty.

He hung up. It was cold in Hornepayne and was likely freezing at night. Northern Ontario was a far cry from Vancouver where frost was usual only in the mountains at this time of year. Purifying frost. It halted the decaying process and cleaned the air. Unfortunately, in Vancouver the rain and dampness provided opportunity for mold and bacteria to grow. Nothing dried in the winter. Oliver once put Gavin's stinking joggers in a plastic bag and tossed them in the fridge's small freezer. Freezing was a proven method of killing the bacteria that caused shoes to smell. Mona went into the compartment for a reason he could not grasp. She did not cook and hadn't prepared much of a meal for them or herself in years, but she found the bag and raised bloody hell, accusing Gavin of trying to poison them. Gavin tried to explain what freezing did to the stench in shoes, but she paid him no more mind than she did Oliver. She'd found something to rant about and ran with it. From then on, Gavin and Oliver hid the bagged shoes in the basement deep freezer under the boxes of chicken breasts and perogies, under all of the food that Mona would never fish out to prepare, for Oliver did all the cooking and the children helped clean up afterward.

In half an hour, passengers milling about the Hornepayne station once more boarded the train, and they were off. The rest of his day was marked by dinner, a shower, a late visit to the courtesy car, and an uneventful game of Scrabble with Shirley.

It would be the last night in his berth. Likely, it would be the last overnight trip he would ever spend on a train. Settled behind the closed curtains, a lot of endings came to Oliver's mind that night. He would perhaps never teach again unless universities or colleges in Toronto were looking for mature sessional instructors. He would have to go back to Vancouver at least once more to settle things with the house and Mona. He hoped it would be sooner rather than later. He was tired of dragging his old life around. Going back to tie up loose ends would be no worse than the hell he had already lived through. If he were lucky and if this was how events played through. So much depended upon the discovery back in Vancouver.

Oliver put on his music, propped his pillows against the window, and leaned back. He closed his eyes and listened to Gluck's *Dance of the Blessed Spirits* from the opera *Orfeo ed Euridice*. He knew the myth of Orpheus well, how Orpheus went to Hades to bring his wife Eurydice back from the dead. Orpheus played his lyre so beautifully that Pluto, god of the underworld, was charmed into letting Eurydice return to the land of the living as long as Orpheus did not look back as he led her out. He did look back though, and that had been the undoing of his plans. Just before Eurydice stepped into the light, she once again became a shade and returned to Hades. Poor doubting Orpheus lost his wife and the future for which he'd hoped.

Oliver was no Orpheus. That he had missed out on that kind of love was a sad thought. He wouldn't die for Mona. He would rather have died than live with her but for Gwen and Gavin. He lived for them, faced hell for them, did what he had to do for them. And soon he would have a grandchild that Mona would never see. He had not missed out on love altogether, but Mona had. She'd lived in her own private hell, and like all unhappy shades of hell, she had been driven to impose her misery on others.

Chapter 16

After Hewitt left for Halifax, Mona went into a spiral of depression. She stayed in her room for days, a week, with Oliver bringing her plates of food from time to time and cleaning up those she barely touched. She did not acknowledge his presence and ate bits of the food only after he left. At the end of a week into her refusal to leave her room, Oliver came in with breakfast to find her standing on a stool in the bathroom with the belt from her robe tied to the shower-curtain rod.

"What are you doing?" He shouted as he pulled her off the stool. He ripped the belt out of her hand and set her on the bed while he ran to get his toolbox. In less than ten minutes, he removed the rod. He went through her closet and took away every belt and sash he found. Lecturing her would do no good, so he threatened her with institutionalization.

"So help me, Mona, I'll call the RCMP and have you committed. You would do this to your children?"

"What children? They don't care about me," she mumbled. "Gavin called me a slut. Did you tell him to say that? My own son called me a slut."

"He apologized for that, Mona. He's a fourteen-year-old boy who was just told his mother had an affair and that his father wasn't who he thought he was. What did you expect him to think? If it's respect you're after, you have to behave like you deserve it, and this won't help," he said gesturing to the bathroom, surprised at the degree of concern her actions had evoked. Oliver left her on the bed and picked up the stool. As he walked out of the room he said, "Take a bath. You'll feel better." But she did not.

Soon, the room began to stink. He tried to cajole her into bathing so he could change the bedding. She refused. At one point, two-and-a-half weeks into her depression, he ran a bath and told her if she didn't get up and bathe, he would carry her to the tub and put her in. She ignored him. He picked her up, shocked by how little she weighed, carried her to the tub, and nightgown and all, placed her in the water. He was sure the neighbors could hear her howl, but he didn't care. He took the shower head and sprayed her hair, squeezed shampoo onto her head as she batted away his hands. In a move that surprised both of them, he ripped her nightgown down the back and pulled it off her. She sat crying hysterically, unable to get out or fight against him any longer.

He toweled her off and got her into her robe. He brought her to the living room while he changed her bedding. Hairdryer in hand, he sat beside her and tried his best to dry her tangled hair. She moaned with each pull of the brush.

Oliver made her tea and a sandwich and watched while she took a few bites and slowly chewed. She curled up on the couch like an exhausted child and fell asleep. If he stopped to watch her as she slept, he would be sucked into her damsel-in-distress whirlpool again, so he left her there and called his doctor.

"Bring her to the emergency room. I'll meet you there. I'll try to have her admitted for an assessment," Dr. Reynolds said.

Oliver refused to hope, but at least his doctor was listening, either that or he was afraid of litigation should Mona actually go through with suicide now that he had been warned. But Oliver would have blamed no one but Mona and himself if her next attempt at suicide was successful.

As she slept, Oliver dressed her as best he could. Whether she really was sleeping or just ignoring him, she did not open her eyes even when he carried her to the cab and strapped her in the seat. He sat beside her and watched that she did not try to flee the car, but he worried that he might lose his concentration and that in a moment of inattention she would spring out the door or awaken from her stupor and attack him. But she did not, not this time. She must truly be in a bad state.

The cab pulled into the emergency bay. Oliver lifted Mona out of the back seat and carried her through to the emergency entrance. Just as he'd promised, Dr. Reynolds was there to meet them. Oliver followed the stretcher up to the psych ward but was told to wait outside in the hall. He faced a pair of locked and deeply scratched and dented doors. *What a sad place*, Oliver thought as he sat in one of the ten plastic chairs lined up along the hall. These green walls were oozing with stories, but he couldn't go deeper into those thoughts now. He had enough on his own plate to deal with. It was eleven in the morning. The children would be home from school at about four. He'd call them then if he'd be late. He was going to stick around and make sure Mona stayed put, make sure she would be assessed. He would answer any questions they had. In fact, he could hardly wait to tell someone in authority just how insane Mona had been making their lives. Someone had to stop her.

The green of the walls reached down every hall and likely into every room. There was no getting away from its contagion. If bilious had a color, it would be the shade of green painted throughout this hospital wing.

In about twenty minutes, Dr. Reynolds came through those ominous gates. "She's been admitted and will be here for at least forty-eight hours. That's how long we can hold her unless she shows signs of self-harm or of harming others. Fill out this form and press the buzzer by the door. Someone will come and take it from you. Go home after that. They'll call you or I'll call you as soon as we know something. She's not talking now, not cooperating at all, so I have no doubt she'll be staying here for at least two days. Get some sleep, Oliver. You look in pretty rough shape yourself."

Oliver shook the doctor's hand and in a voice that lacked conviction and sounded too much like pleading said, "Thank you. Maybe now we'll get to the bottom of this. Maybe we'll get some help and some relief." He *was* pleading. Begging. To be so close to help terrified Oliver because he had been close before only to be horribly disappointed.

After following the doctor's instructions, Oliver left, but with each step he took, the olive walls seemed to undulate, yet he could not bring himself to lean against one for support, feeling if he did, he might sink forever into its thick potage. Life with Mona had brought him to this place, a place where perhaps he belonged as much as she. But there were Gavin and Gwendolyn to consider, so the luxury of tending to himself was put on hold.

Two days later, the hospital called. Mona would be in for another day or two at least since she'd been uncooperative the first two days. The nurse who called asked Oliver if he knew someone named Hewitt, and Oliver did not hesitate to tell her who he was. The nurse told him Mona had named him next of kin.

"Yes, let her call him if that's what she wants. I'm not sure he'll take her calls, but let her try," he said, not caring any more if the whole world knew.

Mona did not call Oliver, nor did she call Gwen or Gavin, not that they were anxious to speak with her. Gavin spent most of his time in sports after school. How fitting that Gavin should take up long-distance running and be so very good at it. Gwen was happy to bring Anna home to hang out in her room for once. Neither of the kids had had that luxury while Mona was around.

After four days, Dr. Reynolds called. "She will be released tomorrow, Oliver. They've completed their assessment, and she seems fit enough. They are not going to hold her."

Shocked in spite of his low expectations, Oliver sat down hard and said, "You've got to be kidding. Are you sure they've tested for everything? Narcissistic Personality Disorder, BPD, the works?"

"Apparently. They are not holding her. The hospital will call with her release time. Also, she's been talking to someone named Hewitt. Are you familiar with him?"

"He was head of psychology at the college where she taught. He's at Dalhousie now," answered Oliver. Then the penny dropped. "Could he have told her how to pass the assessments? How to respond as a normal person would? Oh, God. That's it. He's helped her." Oliver hung up when the doctor agreed she could have been coached. Aside from the initial form he'd filled out, the hospital personnel hadn't questioned Oliver about Mona. Hewitt must have provided answers. She listed Hewitt as the one to contact and to answer any questions about her behavior and her past. She probably told them he was her psychologist.

Anger and resentment should have given him the push he needed to call the hospital and speak with the assessing psychiatrist, but Oliver had had enough of bashing his head against the wall Mona built. He had learned there was no way out, learned to save his energy for what counted—protecting the children. Learned helplessness. Gavin was almost fifteen. He would graduate in two years. Gwendolyn had four years to go. He could retire with full pension in eight. Could he put up with Mona for eight more years? Hewitt was gone, so her threat to take the children and live with Hewitt was weakened although he was obviously still involved. Oliver was named as their father on their birth records. Surely that must count for something.

The children looked crestfallen when he told them Mona would be coming home the following day. He told them after dinner so the news wouldn't spoil their appetite, and early enough in the evening so they might have time to process the news and still get a decent night's sleep.

"Can I go to Anna's after school tomorrow? We've got an exam coming up, and we're studying together," Gwen asked, sure of the answer.

Gavin, too, had cross-country running practice. He would go over to his friend's house for dinner afterward and study there as well. They would both be home by nine. Oliver's sorrow for the pair must have been written on his face. Both of them told him it would be all right. They would stay out of her way and not bother her. They would do whatever they could to keep her from exploding. But it was not their job to protect him, he explained.

"Tell you what. I'll pick you up after practice," he said to Gavin, "and we will get Gwen at Anna's. Let's go out for some pizza, just the three of us before coming back home."

Gavin looked at Oliver with a face that answered for him. "I really do have to study, Dad. It would be better for me to stay at Jeremy's until nine. You can pick me up then."

"Me, too," said Gwen. "Anna and I have planned this for a few days now. We have to be finished at nine though. Maybe we could go out for an ice cream after that."

Oliver would not make it more difficult for them. "Sure thing. I'll pick both of you up at nine and we'll go to Dairyland, just we three." He had to stop reading into their behavior. He had to stop being hyper-vigilant. It was normal for kids their age to spend time with friends, normal and natural. Oh, how she'd screwed-up his mind, his own sanity. How she'd made him worry about every little change in their behavior. Sometimes a kid going to his friend's house after school was just that, plain and simple. Sometimes it was more than that. Trying to figure out the difference was crazy-making.

How often after Mona's most recent attempt at suicide had he wished he had not come into her room at just the right moment. How he wished she had gone through with it. How many problems it would have solved. How much pain it would have alleviated. It wasn't the last attempt she made, however, but Oliver kept saving her, kept doing the right thing, right up until just before he left for Toronto and for good.

Chapter 17

Dance of the Blessed Spirits ended, and Oliver waited for the next piece of music to begin. He'd put the recordings together but he hadn't yet memorized the sequence of play. The notes began. Yes, he knew what it was, Arvo Pärt's *Spiegel im Spiegel*. Mirror in Mirror, the infinity of reflection. When they were youngsters, Gavin and Gwendolyn loved to sit in the wide mirrored window ledge at a downtown Vancouver art gallery. Forget the old masters. They loved looking at themselves multiplied hundreds, thousands of times. They would sit facing each other but look beyond the other's face and into their own reflections, their movements reproduced over and over, backward and forward. They were as much fascinated with the physics of the reflections as by their own never-ending images. Mona would not go with them to see this, not that she would have appreciated the children's curiosity. Their lack of interest in the works of art would have embarrassed her. She would have thought their behavior a reflection on her and would have put a stop to it. She must always appear as though she were a perfect parent, a perfect looking woman, regardless of what lay beneath, regardless of how she behaved within the walls of their home and sometimes without.

"Don't you ever, *ever* talk back to me in front of someone." Mona held Gwendolyn by her upper arm and shook her violently. They stood outside the mall in the parking lot beside the bus stop. Mona had rushed Gwendolyn out, practically dragging the child, to a place where she could really let into her. "You've embarrassed me for the last time, you stupid little idiot. Your behavior reflects on me, and I am not going to let some little gutter snipe make me look bad."

Gwendolyn was crying by the time Oliver and Gavin reached them. Oliver had been waiting outside of the teens-clothing store while Mona shopped with Gwen for back-to-school clothes. He'd let his mind wander as he watched people walking by, normal people, families, parents and children who looked as though they enjoyed each other's company. Gavin ran up to him and woke him from his daydreams. Out of breath he said, "Dad, you better come quick. Mom's got Gwendolyn and she's pretty mad." He filled in the details for Oliver.

They arrived in the middle of Mona's tirade.

"Mona, let her go," Oliver commanded.

"She's my daughter, and I'll discipline her as I see fit." Mona was seething.

"This isn't discipline, Mona. You're angry and taking it out on Gwen. Let her go." Oliver pushed his way between Mona and Gwen, grabbed Mona's wrist and squeezed until she let go of the child's arm.

"You're hurting me!" Mona screamed, having a reason to cause an even bigger scene. "You hurt me!" She moved away holding her wrist up for passers-by to see.

Oliver ignored Mona's drama. "Are you all right," he calmly asked Gwen.

"Just my arm. She didn't hit me. She just yanked me by the arm. I'm okay," said Gwen.

Oliver knew Gwen would downplay anything her mother had done just to avoid a commotion, just to placate her mother. She had red marks around her upper arm that looked like they might turn into bruises. He placed his hand gently over them. They both looked at the bus that would take them home as it turned into the parking lot.

"Would you like to go back into the mall and I'll help you finish shopping, or do you need to go home?" he asked Gwen as Mona kept up her howling.

Gwen looked past him at Mona who was putting on quite a show. She looked at the approaching bus then up at Oliver and said, "I want to finish shopping. Just with you and Gavin."

"Here's bus fare, Mona. Go home. I'll finish shopping with the kids," Oliver said, controlling his hand as he reached out. He could have just as easily shoved her to the ground, but he stopped himself. He kept his tone neutral although everything in him pushed him to add *go, just go. Get out of our lives.* But he did not utter those words out loud. His children were present, and he would do nothing to make things worse for them.

Mona grabbed the money and shoved it in her pocket. "You'd like that, wouldn't you," she screamed. "You get to be the nice guy while I have to put up with her behavior." Mona switched the direction of her rant. "You're not getting off that easy, girlie. Nothing doing. I'm staying here. I have a say in what clothes they buy for school." The bus stopped, and dozens of people disembarked. Mona had her audience.

Oliver took Gwen by the hand, put his other hand on Gavin's shoulder, and the three of them walked back into the mall leaving Mona to be the star of her own drama, a play that ended abruptly when she saw they were leaving and no one else was paying her any attention. Shopping continued with Mona hovering in the background making comments and being critical and cruel. They ignored her as best they could. They were very practiced at pretending she wasn't there, wasn't speaking. How sad they must appear—a husband and two children ignoring the babbling woman behind them. He knew he should include Mona, should ask her opinion, should try much harder to make her part of this family. All the experts had said as much, but what the experts lacked was experience living with her, that no matter how hard he tried, she would turn every kind gesture, every well-meant overture into fuel for combat. The very best he could do at the moment was pretend with all of his shattered heart, mind, and soul that she was not there. He was afraid of what he would do if he turned his attention toward her.

Oliver took a closer look at Gwendolyn's arm when they got home. Bruises ringed her thin bicep. After explaining to Gwendolyn what he was going to do, he called the hotline for reporting child abuse, and a case worker with the Ministry of Child and Family Development arrived at their home several hours later. The case worker, a woman, was about half Oliver's age and seemed inadequate to deal with the situation, at least in his eyes. Mona played the victim role, but in spite of her age, the social worker seemed unaffected by Mona's tears and lies. Not willing to play to an unaccepting audience, Mona marched to her room and locked the door.

"I'd like to speak with Gwendolyn alone," the case worker said. Gwendolyn looked at Oliver with eyes that pleaded with him to stay.

"You'll be fine, Gwen. Just tell the truth. Never be afraid to tell the truth," he said and kissed her on the forehead.

The woman asked Gwendolyn if they could go to her room, so she led the way. In less than half an hour, they both came out. Gwendolyn ran up to Oliver and hugged him. "Can I go to Anna's until dinner?" she asked and danced out the door relieved to be out of the way should another storm hit.

"She's a beautiful child, very articulate, Mr. Eastmund."

"Yes, both my children are very bright in spite of their mother's behavior. I've tried to protect them all of their lives. I've tried to get help for their mother, but she is unwilling to go, and no one can make her. The Ministry is my last hope."

They sat at the kitchen table, and the case worker took notes as they spoke. Within a few minutes, Oliver's worst fears came to fruition.

"Mr. Eastmund, if you cannot protect your children, the Ministry will have to step in to protect them."

"Are you saying the Ministry will remove my children, will take them away from me? Why not remove their mother, make her leave the home? Have her arrested for assault on my daughter?"

"From what I understand, you are not their biological father, and I have to say that leaves you in a pretty precarious position. You can press charges against her, and this will end up in court. Once the court steps in, the Ministry will have no option but to back off. The courts will decide what is best for the children, and I have to say, a stepparent rarely wins in these cases. I did a background check on you and your wife, and it seems you've made some pretty damaging accusations in the past. You abducted the children at one point and the court had to intervene. All of this will go against you."

Oliver knew where this conversation was going. Every muscle in his body was tensing, and it took superhuman strength not to smash the table with his fist and howl to the unresponsive heavens.

"Gwen told me that her mother just squeezed her arm a little too tightly as they were walking to the bus stop, and I doubt that that is enough for a charge of abuse to be laid. It is your choice, but I have to reiterate, if you cannot protect your children, we will. I'll be calling back in a few days to see how things are going."

Oliver said nothing. Even when the woman got up, gathered her notebook and purse and headed for the door, he did not leave his seat. His only consolation was that Mona was not within hearing distance so could not gloat in his face. He didn't have the reserves to control himself if she were to perform her victory parade. For the last time, he chastised himself for making that one early escape attempt when all along he knew there was no way out. Never again would he set up himself and the children for failure. He would ride the nightmare to its bitter end.

The following August, he took the pair shopping without Mona and gave each of them money enough for school supplies and clothing while he sat in the food court, had a coffee, and read. Gavin and Gwendolyn learned to shop within their budget and without the embarrassment that was their mother. Two birds with one stone.

The train gently rocked to the music. Mirror in Mirror—the scene played out over and over again. Mona berated and criticized him and the children, and they in turn ignored her, pretended she wasn't there. Every book Oliver had read, every expert he had spoken with told him the same thing. She needed validation that she was alive and valued. Ignoring her was the worst thing they could do. But Mona could get the help she needed. The children were the helpless ones with a mother who, like a vampire, stole their energy, their self-esteem, their confidence. He knew all too well that Mona's need was unending. No matter how much they gave to her, it would never be enough. He saved his pity for Gwen and Gavin.

Oliver listened to the finale of the soothing music. If Mona had taken only one step toward getting help, he would have supported her with his entire being. Just one step was all it would have taken, and he would have loved her and cared for her with his life. But she never did and never would. It was too late for all of that now. Reflecting on what might have been was too painful, yet he had little choice but to go through it even if the lingering haze of empathy for her and for himself had all but evaporated.

When the hospital called to inform him that he could pick her up, he told the nurse to send Mona home in a cab. The nurse explained that she should be picked up by a family member.

"Why?" he all but shouted into the phone. He didn't care that he sounded angry. He *was* angry. "No one from the hospital bothered to contact me or my children. No one asked us for information or to tell about the hell she has put us through. Maybe the man she's been calling would like to come from Halifax and pick her up. Send her home in a cab or call him. No one from this end is coming to get her." He sounded cruel and uncaring. Maybe he was, but he had learned to be that way in order to survive. Oliver hung up and sat down at his desk. He was exhausted and drained. He put his face in his hands, and because the children weren't home, because Mona wasn't there to gloat at her victory,

Oliver let out a sob, then another, and finally he wept, big and openly. In her own way, she was molding him into the monster she accused him of being.

The cab pulled up in the driveway. Oliver watched her struggle out of the back seat. She was wearing the same green sweater and black pants in which he had dressed her before he had taken her in. The hospital must have issued her toiletries, for he had not provided them. She walked up the front steps as he watched through the window. He did not open the door for her.

"I have no money for the cab," she stated flatly as she slouched toward her room, the room Oliver had scrubbed clean for her. He went out to pay the driver, being careful to take his keys with him. She'd locked him out more than once. Much later, he found out, the hospital had given her a voucher for the cab, but she'd kept it to turn it in for cash or use in the future, perhaps.

Their routines went on as usual, except that Mona was quieter and kept to herself at first. After she'd spent two days in her room without making a sound, Oliver looked to see if she was all right. He half-expected to see her hanging from the hook on her closet door, but she was curled up on the bed, surrounded by piles of clothes, books, food, and dirty dishes.

"What the hell do you want?" she growled.

Oliver closed the door without saying a word. He felt a confusion of relief and disappointment and then disgust at himself for becoming the kind of man who would feel sorry, even for a brief moment, that his wife was still alive.

Chapter 18

At eleven twenty-three, the train stopped for a few minutes in Laforest. In less than ten hours, he would be in Toronto and with his children. He must get all of his emotional baggage behind him before then. He wished he could say he had no regrets except for a bad choice in partners and a tumultuous life. If it were not for him, however, who would have taken care of the children? Would they even be here if Mona hadn't had Oliver to fall back on? How could anyone predict that life would have been better if different choices had been made? The certainty was that they could not have been much worse. That his children had come through and were strong, resilient adults was his only solace. He'd had a hand in that, and it was something, at least. They'd become self-sufficient and independent, and he was proud of that, proud of them. But what they had to go through to get there was unforgiveable.

When Gavin was sixteen, he bought a used lawnmower and went around the neighborhood cutting grass all summer long. Gwendolyn helped by doing some trimming and by sweeping up sidewalks and patios after he'd mowed. Together, they earned money that they quickly deposited into the bank. Autumn brought the opportunity for them to winterize gardens, something they'd learned from Oliver, and in the winter, they shoveled walks on those rare days when it snowed in Vancouver and spread salt on slippery sidewalks. Gwendolyn babysat for his colleagues, and Gavin helped with odd jobs for neighbors. They rarely brought money home since Mona would cajole them out of it or simply take it. Mona had not gone back to work after Gavin was born. She refused. She did not take care of the house or the children. Oliver did that. Yet she insisted upon spending anything she could get her hands on. Oliver paid the bills. He did the grocery shopping with help from Gwen and Gavin because Mona would take the money and spend it on herself. Oliver did the laundry. Gavin, after he bought his mower, did the mowing. Oliver and Gwen tended the flower and vegetable gardens. Oliver did the cooking.

When the children were younger, he'd made their lunches. He stopped making them the night before because Mona would get up in the middle of the night and eat one or the other, so he'd learned to make them in the mornings just before they left for school. As the pair got older, they made their own lunches, just before leaving, no earlier. They also helped Oliver with the housework, dusting and vacuuming while Oliver scrubbed the floors, kitchen, and bathrooms. Everyone took care of his or her own room. Everyone, that is, except for Mona. Her room was a minefield of debris and clutter. Since her attempted suicide and her release from the hospital. Oliver had left her to her own devices.

Mona had become such a recluse that she often surprised them when she came out of her room to join them at the dinner table or to walk through the house looking for something about which to complain.

"I see you've given these two enough money to buy bikes. Pretty expensive-looking ones at that," she said one evening as the three of them were cleaning up the kitchen after dinner.

"We bought them ourselves," said Gwendolyn, who looked like she wished she hadn't after a warning glance from Gavin.

"Bought them yourselves? Where did you get the money? Did you quit school and go to work at McDonalds?" Mona laughed at Gwendolyn's embarrassment.

"I've told you, Mona. The kids have after-school jobs. They've earned every penny. I'm proud of them. You should be, too," Oliver said as he took the clean plates from Gwen and placed them in the cupboard.

"Well, good for you two. Tell me about your bikes. What kind are they? Are they fast? How much did you have to pay for them? It must have taken you forever to earn enough." Mona put on the sweetest voice she had in her repertoire, and although Gavin embraced his mistrust, Gwendolyn's melted away in the warmth of her mother's attention. She babbled away, leaning into Mona as she told all.

"Mine was almost two hundred dollars, but Gavin's was a lot more. Mine has only three speeds. I don't need ten speeds but Gavin does. Dad bought the helmets and the locks. We lock them up wherever we go, even at home in case someone breaks into the garage."

"And you and your brother earned all that money yourselves?"

"Yeah. It was a lot of work cutting grass and doing the trim. I had to do the sweeping up after, but that's why the people asked us back every week. We did more than just cut the grass. I also babysit, and Gavin does odd jobs." Gwendolyn reveled in the attention. Mona sat and listened. She placed two hands on Gwen's waist, looking up into her daughter's eyes with a face that appeared interested. It masked a sinister plan and Oliver knew what that plan was. He did not want to explain their mother's deviousness to the children if he didn't have to. Nor did he want to get Mona riled up by having Gwen and Gavin bring their bikes into their rooms at night. Not yet. He'd have to catch her in the act and take the brunt of her anger before taking that step.

Oliver kept vigil for three nights running, catching up on sleep with naps during the day and after dinner. He kept his office light on late into the night to make it look as though he was working. At eleven thirty, he turned it off, checked the children's doors to make sure they were locked, glanced toward the light coming from under Mona's door, and as stealthily as he could, he moved to the garage to keep watch over the bikes. On the fourth night, as he made himself comfortable on an old chaise lounge, he heard a car pull up in front of the house. Voices cut through the darkness. The garage door lifted as Oliver hid behind the clutter of stored furniture and bins. He watched the silhouettes of Mona and a stranger as they moved toward the bikes.

"We paid over six hundred dollars for the man's bike and three for the woman's. All we are asking is five hundred for both," Mona lied.

"Seems a little steep," the man answered. "Are you sure they're not stolen?"

Oliver stepped out from the shadows and said, "Not yet, they aren't. These bikes were bought by my son and daughter who worked for a year and a half earning the money. What you see here is their mother trying to sell their bikes out from under them. They're not for sale."

"Geeze lady, your own kids' bikes? Now I see why you wanted me to meet you here so late. What were you going to do, cut the locks with those bolt cutters?" he said as Mona grabbed them from beside the door. "I'm out of here. Thanks for wasting my time." To Oliver he said over his shoulder as he turned to go, "Sorry, man. I swear I didn't know. Good luck with this one," he said as he nodded toward Mona. He walked to his car and sped off.

"Yes, Mona. What were you going to do? You really are messed up." He stepped back as she raised the bolt cutters and lunged toward him. Mona let out a roar as she swung at Oliver's head. She missed. She tried to raise the tool again but it was caught in the webbing of the chaise and the entire thing came up with it. She bashed the aluminum chair on the concrete floor again and again making such a racket that both Mrs. White and the McHughs, who lived on the other side of them, turned on their outdoor lights.

"What's going on out there," Ted McHugh called out.

"Mind your own damn business," Mona screamed at him.

Ted turned to his wife and said loud enough for all to hear, "It's just the crazy woman next door doing her usual shit."

Oliver couldn't help but say in the silence that followed Ted's comment something he knew he should not, but he, too, was only human. He, too, had a breaking point.

"You need help, Mona, and if you do not get it soon, I will leave you. When the children are gone and all of our debts, your debts, are paid, I will leave. Remember this. It is not a threat. It's a promise, and you must prepare for it."

Mona muffled a shriek with her hand. She dropped the bolt cutters and turned toward the house. Oliver quickly disentangled them from the chair and carried them with him. He shut the garage door and followed her. She'd locked the house door behind her, but Oliver had his keys and let himself in. He would not give her the opportunity to take her rage out on the kids. But Mona screamed loudly enough to rouse both of them.

"You give those two money," she bellowed, "but I don't have enough to live on." She accused Oliver, alternately directing her barbs at the children and at him, pointing into his chest as though she would stab him through the heart. "As if they deserve it more than I."

"You get as much as we can afford, certainly more than they or I do," Oliver stated flatly. He had outlined their budget for her fifty times or more, explaining how they had to pay off her debts as well as keep the house running and put aside funds for the children's education, but it all fell on deaf ears. Each time, she tore up the sheets Oliver had so carefully prepared. Reality was negotiable as far as she was concerned. Facts meant nothing.

"I need more money," Mona screamed over and over again.

Oliver put the bolt cutters in his office, afraid he might be tempted to swing them at her. She followed him, but he turned and walked into her, backing her out the door and shutting it behind him. He was careful to keep his eyes on her the entire time.

"I give you as much as we can afford," he said calmly and softly. "How much more do you need?"

"I need my own money, money I don't have to tell you about," she shouted.

"Then I suggest you get a job. Get a job and keep every penny of the money you earn. I won't stop you. I won't ask anything from you. But tell me, just what do you need the extra money for? I'm curious. Is it to buy a plane ticket to go see Hewitt?"

"None of your damn business," she hissed.

"If that's the case, I'll see what I can do about getting the money to buy the ticket for you."

Mona paused, as much surprised that he would make such an offer as she seemed contemplating taking him up on it. It didn't take her long to turn on him. "You'd like that, wouldn't you? You'd get a lawyer and go to court saying I abandoned my children, wouldn't you?" Mona gave a low chuckle. "Nice try, Oliver. You're catching on, finally. But I'll always be a few steps ahead of you, you bumbling idiot. Are you going to sleep in the garage forever? I'll get the money somehow, and when I do, I'll spend it on anything I like. I don't have to answer to you." She walked away from him and slammed the door to her room.

The bikes were safe that night. He had the bolt cutters. After that, the kids brought their bikes into their rooms at night if Mona wasn't around. If she was, Oliver brought them in and kept them in his room. But little by little, Mona was selling things from the house, small things like vases and books. One day he came home, and the living room curtains were gone. She was gathering up money bit by bit. It was not normal for a father to install deadbolt locks on the outside of his and his children's bedroom doors, but it was necessary. They had to lock their rooms when they weren't at home. Mona would stop at nothing. She would sell their very beds given the chance. Perhaps it would be better to give in to her than it was to sit in gut-churning anticipation. Let her do as she will. But there was little money to spare.

It was all sound and fury signifying nothing. She would not go to her lover. She spent everything she could get on herself—a laptop, clothes, makeup, lunches and dinners out, going out nights. Nothing on the children. Nothing on the rest of the house. She took cabs out for the evening, not telling anyone where she was going and no one bothering to ask. She was just a boarder, a free-loading occupant. Not a parent. Not a wife. Oliver could live with that, and he did until Gavin went to university and Gwen followed.

Chapter 19

At one seventeen in the morning, the train stopped. Sudbury Junction. A few people stood outside the station waiting for a couple to step down from the train. When the couple joined the group, they embraced one another and divided the suitcases among them. He watched them walk past the station to the lone car in the brightly lit parking lot. He could see nothing beyond. The group, family or friends, jostled and grinned, happy to be together. Gwen, Gavin, Theresa, and he would feel the same when they met in Union Station. Would they meet him where the train pulled up, he wondered, or would he have to make the trek into the train station and meet them in that vaulted, echoing place? He had been in Union Station often when visiting years past. The Go Train and subway lines stopped there, and he'd walked the maze of tunnels lined with fast-food kiosks and newsstands, shoe-repair shops and luggage stores. He loved to stand in the main corridor under the high glass roof. He was amazed that so many people rushed through, never looking up, never appreciating the architecture of the grand hall. Then again, perhaps he, too, would become so accustomed to it that he would no longer be astonished by its grandeur, much like he had taken the ocean and mountain views in Vancouver for granted. It is true that people do not appreciate what is so close to them until it's gone. He'd loved his garden, but that also came to an end.

It would be a sleepless night, sleepless and tortured.

Gavin had the results of all his university applications sent to him via a post office box. Oliver thought perhaps he could use his own box at the university, but it was not secure. Mona had more than once gone into the mailroom and rifled through his cubbyhole looking for checks. He assumed that was what she was after. Perhaps she was simply snooping for information. She was convinced, obsessed with the idea that he was cheating on her. He had to laugh over that, a kind of gallows humor, since, in spite of her treatment of him and in spite of his own need for love and companionship, Oliver had remained faithful. It was more the result of his own fear and lack of trust in his judgment than an abundance of virtue. He had chosen Mona, after all, and he was convinced that even worse may be out there.

Gavin was accepted at every university to which he applied. He chose York because of the reputation of their law program. But just before Gavin left for university, Mona raised her monster. They expected nothing less and were prepared for her.

"Where's he going?" she snarled at Oliver as they brought in two large suitcases picked up at a second-hand store. She turned on Gavin. "Where in the hell do you think you're going?"

Gavin ignored her and shut his bedroom door before she could enter. Of course, that sent her into a rage, and she screamed while pounding on the door with both fists.

"Gavin has been accepted at a university, and he is leaving. He flies out tomorrow. You will just have to accept it, Mona. He's not a child." Oliver's monotone voice juxtaposed hollowly against Mona's rage.

"What university? Why does he have to leave home when he could go here for free? What a waste of money. Is he studying something that isn't offered here?" Bit by bit, she lowered her voice as Oliver continued to explain, his voice calm and steady.

"He is studying law, Mona. He's going to be a lawyer, and he is not telling you where he's going. He's leaving because of you, because he can't stand the chaos anymore. Gwendolyn will too, I expect. Before you get it into your head to ask, no one knows where Gavin is going except me, and I'm not telling you."

"A lawyer. Whose bright idea was that, as if I had any doubt," Mona said as she turned her head toward him and narrowed her eyes. It had been a few months since she'd flown at him, but Oliver was ready. He took a step back, and she laughed. She glared but did nothing. Mona walked to her room and closed the door quietly for once. He could hear her muffled sobs as she cried into her pillow. He'd said too much. It would have been enough just to tell her that her son was leaving. The unkind part of him, the monster in him, needed to twist the knife, and who could blame him. The truth was the truth. But she was still Gavin's mother, and somewhere deep inside of her perhaps there was a kernel of affection after all. Maybe some acknowledgement of just what she had done to Gavin, to Gwen, to this family had been touched upon and recognized.

It was short lived. The sobs turned to screams, the screams to rage and curses. Oliver gathered Gavin's laundry from the basement as quickly as he could and shoved the basket into Gavin's hands. Oliver stood before the door blocking Mona's charge, taking the full brunt of her head into his chest. Had he not grabbed her shoulders to lessen the blow, they both would have fallen into Gavin's room.

"Lock the door, son," Oliver said as Gavin shut the door.

In a moment, however, Gavin opened the door and said to his father, "Not this time. This time I can fight my own battle."

"All my life I've watched you rant and rave like a damn lunatic. I was scared to death of you when I was little. What kind of parent terrifies her own kid? Maybe Dad thinks you're mentally ill, but you're just plain evil. A selfish, fucking bully. A monster. I hate you. I have hated you most of my life and I can't wait to leave you behind and never see you again. As soon as I leave, I'm changing my name. You will never see me again. I want nothing to do with you. You are dead to me."

Oliver did not intervene. He watched his son as he threw all he had at Mona. Gavin's tears mocked his vehemence. Oliver understood the brokenhearted love behind the words, the years of hoping for Mona's love, any show of affection. Oliver felt that familiar pain and knew this was Gavin's last attempt to get through to her and to make her see him. His need for love. His need to love.

Gavin's words pushed her back, pushed her into her room with Gavin following until he saw the filth, until the stench smacked him in the face. His mouth fell open. He had never been inside his mother's room, not since he was a toddler. The evidence of her madness was undeniable. No one could live like this and be sane. Gavin backed out. Mona stood silent in her room. Oliver closed her door.

"Let's get your bags packed, son. We'll take your things to Jeremy's place and leave for the airport early tomorrow morning. Tonight, the three of us will go out for a farewell dinner. Invite Jeremy to come along, that's fine."

Gwen, Gavin, Jeremy and Oliver went to the best restaurant Oliver could afford that night, and amid tears and laughter, Gavin's freedom was celebrated.

Jeremy was sworn to secrecy about Gavin's university. Not even his parents knew. It was best that way. Mona could not manipulate them.

"I swear, too," said Gwen as she held up her right hand. "On pain of death, I won't tell a soul."

"You can join me in two years, Gwen. You'll get a scholarship and then you'll be free. Come to Toronto, to York. We'll live it up in T.O.," Gavin offered as an incentive for Gwen to stay strong and not give in to their mother's conniving.

Twice in the two years that followed, Gwen and Oliver flew to Toronto to visit Gavin. Both times they told Mona they were going to a cottage up in Northern B.C. They rented a car for the trip to the airport just to make their lie more believable. But Mona said she thought something fishy was going on.

"What sixteen-year-old goes camping with her father? Shouldn't you be going out with boys your own age?" she said. "Come to think of it, maybe you're not interested in boys. I've never seen you go out with one or bring one home. Are you a lesbian? It's okay if you are. Safer that way." Mona laughed at a humiliated Gwen. She'd never brought a boy home. Why would she? How could she? For that matter she'd never brought any friend home except for Anna that brief time when Mona was hospitalized. But Gwen did not have Gavin's courage or his outrage. She shrank from her mother's venomous words, but she kept her promise to her brother. Secrecy was both her protection and her way out.

Oliver and Gwen spent two weeks with him the first year Gavin was in Toronto. Gavin took classes year-round and had a part-time job as a lifeguard at a community center. They stayed in Gavin's cramped bachelor apartment and felt more comfortable there than they had ever felt at home in Vancouver. Oliver cooked meals for Gavin to freeze and stocked him up with toiletries and cleaning supplies, staples and houseware. Before they left, Oliver went over a budget with Gavin and mapped out how much money he could offer his son over and above his scholarship. Oliver had set money aside, enough to help a little.

Gavin did well. He seemed happy in his surroundings and engaged with his studies. When Gwen and Oliver came the second year, Gavin introduced them to his girlfriend, Theresa.

"I am so happy to finally meet you, Mr. Eastmund," Theresa said as she held out her hand. She looked straight into Oliver's eyes and had a sure and strong handshake. "Gavin has spoken about you non-stop, both of you. Gwen, you look so much like Gavin. You are clearly brother and sister."

How much had Gavin told her? Did she know that Gavin was not his biological son? Oliver was hesitant to feel good about Gavin's new relationship, but as the days went by, Theresa grew on him. She was cheerful but not sappy. She called Gavin on some of his clumsier moves such as forgetting his shift at the pool or leaving a coffee ring on a midterm paper he had yet to hand in. She called him on these things, but then it was over. No shouting. No berating. No animosity. Not from her and not from Gavin. Both could speak their minds without a blow up.

Oliver was the one who cringed when Theresa said, "This dish is filthy. Wash it again," and dropped the plate back into the dishwater.

Gavin replied, "Picky, picky, picky. What's a little food gunk between friends?" and rewashed the plate.

Oliver and Gwen were both on the alert when Gavin told Theresa to get her freezing feet off him while they watched television. Theresa laughed, put socks on and planted her feet right back on Gavin's lap. Oliver looked at Gwen and they exchanged their worried looks for smiles. The affection between Gavin and Theresa was obvious, not showy but calm and steady. They made no demands of each other. Each had friends and activities that broadened their lives. Their timetables for classes and Gavin's work schedule were posted on the fridge, and they checked with each other before making plans. Often, they went out on their own, yet neither expressed outrage or jealousy. They were comfortable with each other, comfortable with themselves. It took about a week for Oliver and Gwen to accept that this was what normal looked like. Normal give and take. Natural camaraderie. Sane behavior. It only took a few hours back in Vancouver and back home to miss the comforts of life without Mona.

When his daughter was ready to leave, Oliver settled Gwen into Gavin's old bachelor suite along with a roommate, Shannon, whom Gavin had vetted for her in order to fray expenses. Gavin had moved in with Theresa. Gwen had won a scholarship and had her choice of several universities, but as planned chose to follow her brother to York. Much to Oliver's surprise, she decided to study psychology. He thought she would prefer to get away from dealing with insanity.

"I know what you mean, Dad, but if I could understand what makes people act the way they do, I might not have such tangled feelings about her. Knowledge is power, after all." Gwen had always been more inclined to forgive Mona. Oliver was not convinced that this was the best way to go about detaching from life with that kind of mother, but he loved his daughter, had faith in her intelligence and ability, and more than that, he respected her right to choose for herself how she would deal with what life had dumped on her. Perhaps Oliver needed to focus more on his own escape. His children had clearly made their choices.

Oliver had secreted his daughter away in the late afternoon of Gwen's last mid-August days in Vancouver. Mona was not home, unaware of her daughter's plans. Mona was a ghost in the house for the most part, and that worked well for all. Oliver left a note telling her they'd gone camping and would be back in a week, a shorter time than usual, which would certainly alert Mona to something else going on. Much later, Oliver learned that she went to Gwen's friend and made small talk with Anna and her mother until she got out of the girl information about the scholarship, nothing else.

But Mona knew what was up. She was not stupid even if she was absent from their lives. With no one upon whom to take out her rage, she attacked the one thing she knew Oliver loved most next to Gwen and Gavin.

The night Oliver returned, Mona was stretched out on the couch in the living room reading a book. She looked up at him and smiled.

"Gwen all set up?" she asked sweetly.

"Yes, she starts university in a week. She won a scholarship, just like Gavin. Smart kids."

"You lied when you wrote you two were gone camping."

"I didn't want a scene like the one we had with Gavin. I was determined to make Gwen's departure drama free, so yes. I lied, but you have to admit you brought it on yourself."

"And you've brought something on yourself as well, my dear."

"What's that, Mona. What have you done? Nothing would surprise me, nothing at all." But he was wrong. The next morning in the bright sunshine, Oliver took his coffee out to the garden. He stopped on the porch and surveyed the carnage Mona had inflicted in his absence. All of the raised beds were torn apart and the plants and soil scattered across the lawn. The rose bushes—red, white, pink, and coral-colored roses so tenderly planted for his mother by

Gavin—were lying with their roots exposed, all the leaves dried and shriveled. Every dwarf fruit tree was sawed off at ground level, and each plant—daisies, rudbeckia, sedum, hydrangea, lavatera, and all the annual plants he had so carefully placed to fill in gaps in color, shape, and space—uprooted and dried out from days of exposure in the summer heat.

He could barely breathe. Surely now he could leave her. She could not find Gavin and Gwen. They were safe. If he walked away now, he would have to share his income with her. She had not worked a day since before Gavin's birth. She would go after his pension as well. It would be a small price to pay for peace of mind, for freedom from chaos. But there were the outstanding debts, thousands, that would take him four more years to pay off if he kept up at the pace he was going. He could not do that on half his salary. The house was rented at an extremely low rate from the university. He could not find a bachelor apartment in Vancouver for what he was paying in rent for this house. She had done what she could to destroy him. But as he looked out across the devastated yard, he felt oddly free. This was the last thing he cared about, and she had taken it from him. She could do nothing more than take his life, and that, at this point, seemed like a magnificent end to enslavement. He finally managed a deep breath and exhaled slowly, a sad honoring of a once beautiful place.

"Oh, Oliver. I tried to stop her." Mrs. White leaned on the fence between their yards. "I even called the police, but they said the property belonged to the university and they would have to be the ones to lay charges. I didn't want to get you into trouble with them, so I didn't make that call. All your hard work. It was so beautiful. What is wrong with her? Why would she destroy her own home?"

Oliver shook his head. He didn't have an answer for her or for himself. All he knew was that he was tired of looking for answers where none existed. He went back inside, got dressed, and went out to the garden to rake up the mess and make it as presentable as possible. The work kept him busy, kept him from retaliating. The patio furniture was gone, likely sold. The make-shift barbecue was flattened beyond recognition. Four years. He could retire with full pension in four years, and in four years, every debt to which his name was attached would be paid. Could he manage that long? He'd lived in hell thus far, and he could put in another four years. Then, maybe, he could afford to move to Toronto and live near his children.

Such wishful thinking. Did she think that with everything and everyone he cared about gone, he would turn his attention and affection on her and her alone? How could she believe that when he'd told her clearly and unequivocally that he would leave her when the children and debts were gone? Had he encouraged her in some way that was as sick as she? Perhaps she saw the minuscule ember of love almost burned out, almost invisible under the ashes of their existence. He had believed only he knew it hibernated there in the depths of his being ready should the merest breeze of hope fan it to life. After all of this, he said to himself as he surveyed the ruins, even after all of this.

Chapter 20

Parry Sound, and it was four thirty-three in the morning. He had not slept. Oliver tried to get comfortable in the closed-in berth, but he feared that if he fell asleep now, he would miss the chance to shower before breakfast and their arrival in Toronto. Unlike at the beginning of his journey, now the car and berths were full. It seemed too early to get up. He would likely disturb others as he clambered about, climbing down from his berth and gathering his clothing. While he avoided making friends, he did not relish making enemies, either. He'd wait and try not to go back to the past but focus on Gwen and Gavin and on how life would be from this point forward.

Gwen was in graduate school, a Ph.D. candidate. She was as focused on her studies as Gavin had been on his. She, too, worked as a lifeguard part-time, and Oliver contributed what he could. Neither of them ever complained about his lack of financial support. They seemed happy to be making their own way. Oliver, too, would be content with whatever space Gavin and Theresa had created for him. One room would be sufficient, but Theresa said they'd redone the coach house for him. The coach house had long ago been converted to a garage, a huge thing that could house four cars, if needed. If he had a small apartment above, it would be more than enough, more than he deserved. And the new baby was something to which he looked forward. New life. New hope. Just one more hurdle to jump and, if all went well, he would be a man unfettered, a man who could give his love freely and accept love in return—uncomplicated love, pure and without fear.

When the train started up again, it was just after five o'clock. Now that he would be in Toronto sooner than anyone from Vancouver could arrive to confront him, Oliver made one last phone call to Mona. No matter what had happened back in Vancouver, he would be found out. Why pretend that he could hide? Even when he changed his name, he would be discovered. By filing income tax, he would be traceable. He would rather get it over with sooner than later.

"Okay, Mona," he began. "I guess you are not going to answer. The train arrives in Toronto in a few hours, and I will call you once I get there. If you don't answer or don't get in touch with me, I'll call Mrs. White to check on you. Better yet, I'll call the police so Mrs. White won't have to be involved. I'm aware of how you feel about her. We've got to settle things, Mona."

Oliver was first using the shower room and finished dressing before a single person lined up at the door. He checked his berth to make sure he had everything packed safely into his one small case and backpack. He'd be going back to Vancouver for the rest of his things, but so much of his future depended upon what was discovered there. He went to the hospitality car to make a pot of coffee and wait for the call to breakfast. Shirley was not there. He hoped he would have the chance to say goodbye since in all likelihood, he would not see her again. She had no idea how much she'd helped him on this journey, and while he would not go into detail with her, he did owe her at least a farewell. Oliver took out a book and within minutes of reading, he fell asleep with his dreams wandering back to the last years with Mona.

It was impossible. He could not stay in the same house with her for another minute. Although she could not get into his office and bedroom, she had access to everything outside of it. Every jacket hanging in the front closet, every pair of shoes and boots there as well disappeared or were cut into strips or torn apart. She left the heap of rags in the middle of the kitchen floor where he was sure to find them. He was furious, but she was gone, not returning until the early hours of the morning when he was asleep.

If he were to have any future at all, employment for the next few years would be necessary, but he could not live with Mona, nor could he afford to rent another apartment near campus, if there were any left to rent. Vancouver's vacancy rate was less than zero. Although he was reluctant to drag a colleague into the insanity of his life, in his exhaustion and hopelessness, he approached Felix Eppert, a man with whom he had taught for most of his career. Felix and most of the department were aware of Mona and her treatment of him and the children ever since Brenda Macintyre had witnessed her suicide threat so many years ago and the annual welcome-back gatherings where Mona had barely hidden her malevolence. Oliver had felt the looks of pity and noted the hush of conversation when he walked into rooms. But Felix was more than encouraging when Oliver asked if it were possible for him to rent a room from him and his wife. Oliver moved in that evening. He had few belongings left after Mona's rampage. Most of his books had long ago been moved to his office at the university, so there were only his clothes, toiletries and laptop.

All seemed well for the first week, but then Mona began to show up in his classes, sitting in the back row of the lecture theater, staring at him with intermittent looks of menace and seduction. He finally cornered her after class and threatened her with security if she showed up again, would have them watch for her if she set foot on campus. She stopped coming, but Oliver could not rest easy. She would find some other way to destroy his peace.

Two days later, a dead bird lay on the front porch of Felix Eppert's home. Felix chalked it up to a neighborhood cat, but Oliver's hackles raised. The next day, small blue plastic bags of dog shit sat neatly in the center of each step demanding attention and eliminating any doubt about the deliberateness of the act. In the small hours of the morning on the day that followed, a rock smashed through the picture window of the house. Oliver insisted upon cleaning up the mess and paying for the window to be repaired, but in as gentle a way as possible, Felix asked Oliver if, perhaps, he might find somewhere else to stay.

Humiliated and defeated, Oliver had but one choice if the Epperts were going to be free of Mona's attacks. The law could not help him. There was no proof that Mona was to blame. She was smart enough to ensure no fingerprints were on the bags or the rock, smart enough to make sure no one saw her. Even if he moved elsewhere, until she followed him and found his new residence, she would continue to torment the Epperts. But there was nowhere to go. He couldn't eliminate their debts and pay rent elsewhere, and his colleagues, as concerned as they were, were avoiding him, especially Brenda Macintyre. She knew first-hand how insane his life was and would not subject her family to Mona's threats.

No choice remained if the Epperts were to be protected. He and Mona could live as strangers in the same house as long as he could lock his belongings in his room and stay away from home as much as possible. His mantra became *When the debts are paid...when the debts are paid...* It was the only way he could keep going.

Oliver awoke when the steward tapped him on the shoulder and announced breakfast. It was eight o'clock. They would arrive in Toronto in an hour and a half.

Shirley was seated at the table when he arrived. "I thought I'd miss saying goodbye," he said.

Shirley smiled at him. "I would have looked for you. You wouldn't get off this train without me wishing you well. Besides, the train doesn't leave for Montreal for a few hours. I plan on getting out and walking around downtown for a while."

With just a twinge of nervousness, Oliver said, "In that case, you'll have a chance to meet my kids." He was sure Gwen, Theresa, and Gavin would be there to meet him, but would anyone else? Everything could fall apart at the last minute, and a further witness to the absurdity that was his life was unwelcome. He could deal with complications should they arrive, but upsetting anyone else would be unfair. Shirley seemed steady, sturdy enough, though. She seemed the kind of person who could roll with whatever came up.

"I'd like that," she said.

Oliver stood holding his luggage, eager to disembark. He peered through the window and saw few people on the platform. It looked as though he would have to find the kids in the station, in the main corridor at the end beneath the clock as they had discussed. He stepped off the train and waited for Shirley. Two uniformed police officers stood watching the passengers, questioning a few from time to time. When they stopped Donald Montgomery, he turned and pointed to Oliver. Shirley walked up to him just as the officers approached.

"Oliver Eastmund?" one of the officers asked.

"Yes, I'm he." His years of practice at keeping a neutral face served him well at this point.

"Mr. Eastmund, we need to speak with you. Privately," the officer said, nodding to Shirley. She stepped a short distance away and turned to watch. A few others paused in their rush to get to the stairs that would take them down into the station.

"What is it? Has something happened to my children? Are they all right? They're meeting me here. In the station." He tried to show a degree of nervousness, a bit of babbling to cover up. *Keep it together*, he told himself. *If this is to work, keep it together*.

"Do you live at 2311 Westview Road in Vancouver?" one officer asked.

"Yes, at least I did. My wife and I are divorcing, and I'm here to live near my children or at least to see about it."

"Mr. Eastmund, I'm sorry to inform you that there has been an incident with your wife, in Vancouver. Perhaps you would rather go into the station and be with your children while we explain."

Oliver said nothing. He looked intently in the man's face for several seconds. The man was serious, but not unkind looking. The gray station shifted around Oliver. *Free! I'm finally free!* Almost losing his balance, he reached for the stern officer who grabbed his arm and held him steady. He was ready to hear what he already knew. Finally, he said, "No, tell me now. I'll break it to my children." These were crucial moments. He had to be careful. All had gone so wrong with police and lawyers, doctors and social workers in the past. He had to keep his mind straight and his thoughts clear. He had to act the part.

The officer looked around and caught the attention of his partner then led Oliver away from the train and the disembarking passengers. "Mr. Eastmund, it appears as though your wife attempted to take her own life. She's in very serious condition in…" and he looked at his notebook, "…the hospital at BCU."

Oliver closed his eyes. She's not dead. How? How had she survived? *Think. Think before you speak*, he repeated to himself. "How? How did she…do it?" he asked, his eyes opening after the platform stopped reeling.

"It appears she tried to hang herself. If it wasn't for the postman who noticed the opened front door, she might have succeeded."

Oliver was no longer acting. He was horrified, but not because Mona was dead—because she wasn't. "Where? At the house, yes, but where did she…?" he finally asked.

"The garage. After the postman called into the house and there was no answer, he looked through the door of the garage, and she was there. If you come with me, we'll meet with your son and daughter, Gavin and Gwendolyn, isn't it?" he said as he looked again at his notes.

"Yes, and my son's wife, Theresa. They're all here, I believe."

The two officers and Oliver walked toward the stairs. Shirley was waiting nearby, and she passed Oliver her card. "I'll be coming back through Toronto in a couple of weeks. Give me a call. I hope everything is all right."

"Thank you, Shirley. Thank you," was all he could say before one of the officers stopped to get her name and number.

"We may have a few questions for you afterward," he said to her, and he also took a card. He held Oliver by the arm, perhaps afraid he would throw himself down the chiseled stone steps or try to run, but his legs shook and he stumbled on the first step. It wasn't an act, not this time. He could not believe that she was still alive. Never had anything in their lives together gone as hoped for. Now this. The officer caught him and helped him maneuver the remaining steps.

As they left the stairwell and walked into the station, Gavin, Gwen, and Theresa were there with huge welcoming smiles spread across their faces. Gwen gave a small jump of joy when she saw him, but their expressions sobered quickly when they saw the officer holding their father's arm and a second policeman following behind.

"It's all right. I'm fine, and I'm happy to see that you three are okay. The officers came to tell me that there has been an incident with your mother." He paused giving them time to shift their thoughts. "She tried, unsuccessfully, to end her life and is in serious condition in the hospital. I have to go back immediately. Gavin, will you drive me to the airport?"

Gavin and Gwendolyn reached out to their father. Theresa joined them. They formed a circle and put their heads together.

"Oh, Dad," Gwendolyn said. She did not cry, nor did Gavin. It was Oliver's one defeated sob that echoed in the cavernous hall.

After the family broke their embrace, the officer in charge said he had a few questions for Oliver. He asked if he would like to answer them here or come down to the station. Gavin, suddenly the serious lawyer, told the officers he would act as his father's solicitor and asked Oliver what he would prefer.

"Let's get it over with, Gavin. I've got to get back to see what I can do, how I can help."

His son, daughter, and daughter-in-law looked at each other. Oliver read their expressions. *Had he not done enough for her?* they seemed to ask. Oliver hoped the officers could not see what he saw or rather what was not apparent. They seemed very concerned, very worried, but Oliver knew their anxiety was for him.

They walked together to the station's security offices and sat in a sparsely-furnished room. The questions seemed harmless enough to Oliver—when was the last time he saw his wife? What time did he leave the house? Did he say goodbye to his wife? How many times had he called her during his trip? Why hadn't he contacted a neighbor or friend when she did not answer his calls?

Oliver said he had left after his wife had begun another argument, one of many they had had over his leaving. He left the house and walked to the bus stop at about two in the afternoon. He had shouted goodbye to her, telling her he would call. He asked if they found the money and the note that he'd left for her, and the officers said that both were accounted for.

"Yes, I closed the front door behind me," he repeated to the question the officer had asked twice already.

Again, the officers looked at each other.

"Did you lock it?"

"No. I actually thought of opening it again to say goodbye one more time, but then I stopped myself. I didn't want to face another argument. I didn't lock it. She was there, so I saw no need. I closed it and left. I stopped and talked to my neighbor, Mrs. White, as I passed. She was out in her front garden. And I walked away to catch my bus. I asked her if the mail had come, but it hadn't."

"How far away was the bus stop?"

"About a ten-minute walk."

"Did you see the postman on your way?"

"No, I didn't see the postman. I was disappointed that he was so late. He usually comes around noon. I'd hoped to check the mail before I left, but he was too late. I had to leave." *Slow down. Don't ramble. Tell them only what they are asking for.*

"Did he often come late?"

"On occasion. Not often. Not with any regularity."

Again, the officer asked him why he had not called a friend or neighbor after Mona hadn't returned his calls. In his messages he said he would, if she didn't answer.

"We have no friends, at least none that would get involved or confront Mona. She had some serious problems. I tried to get her help, but no one would listen to me." Oliver looked over to his children. Both Gwen and Gavin were stoic and stone-faced. Theresa, however, was wiping away tears. Had Gavin filled her in on their wretched lives, or was she crying, as one might, for a woman who'd had a tragedy?

"I was going to give Mrs. White a call, but Mona hates her, and she dislikes Mona." Oliver paused. "Mona could get quite irate, and I didn't want to expose Mrs. White to Mona's anger, not while I wasn't there to mitigate the situation."

"Did you tell your neighbor that you were taking the train to Toronto?"

Oliver hesitated long enough to consider his answer. If he let slip that, Gavin and Gwen had not seen or spoken to their mother in years and Mona had no idea where they were and that he would never have revealed where they lived, he would be opening a can of worms that could cast even more suspicion on himself and maybe on them. At the time, he could have told Mrs. White the truth about where he was going without fear of Mona finding out. But out of force of habit he had told her no more than that he was going to visit them and had never mentioned Toronto.

"I'm not sure," he lied. "I might have. I can't remember if I did or not." Oliver forced himself not to look at either Gwen or Gav.

Gavin asked, "Why all the focus on whether or not the front door was closed?"

The officer who had asked most of the questions answered. "The postman said it was open when he got there, that's all. Thank you for your time, Mr. Eastmund. Those are all the questions we have for now. You are heading back to Vancouver? Someone will get in touch with you there. We may have more questions for you, so make yourself available."

Oliver handed them his card and Gavin did the same. The officers walked them to the main corridor then left as Gwendolyn threw her arms around Oliver. She cried as he held her tightly, and he felt not her weight but that of his old millstone grow heavier than it had ever been. She was alive. Mona had survived. He would never be free.

Chapter 21

Oliver landed in Vancouver sixteen hours after his ordeal in Toronto. He'd waited half a day at Pearson Airport, hardly a restful delay. He'd dozed a little on the plane, but it was not enough to lift his exhaustion. Aside from the brief nap in the air, he'd been awake for over twenty-four hours. Too tired to manage the sky train and busses, Oliver took a cab home, no matter the cost.

Mona had not had time to destroy the house, but he half expected to walk into utter chaos. It was eerily neat, all except for Mona's bedroom, he was sure. He would scour that room another day. Today, he did not open her door. It was too late to see Mona in the hospital. Tomorrow would be soon enough. Utterly fatigued by disappointment as well as everything else, Oliver dropped onto the living room sofa. Poor Gavin and Theresa. The look on their faces when he insisted on being driven straight to the airport without stopping to see the home they had created for him was pure dismay. All he managed to do was sign the papers for his name change, papers that Gavin handed to him while he waited in the airport. It was the only thing Gavin could do for him, and the only thing Oliver could give his son at the time. He had not told the police of his pending name change. He'd learned the less said, the better when it came to those who saw themselves as authorities.

In spite of all of his planning and what he saw as macabre serendipity, Oliver had loosely held on to the slight hope that he could escape. Fool that he was, he had set aside his certainty that Mona would move heaven and hell to keep him in her grasp. Now she was dead weight, in a near vegetative state, able only to sit in a wheelchair, the nurse he'd spoken with told him. But she was not able to speak. They were not sure how much she could comprehend, but she was certainly unresponsive to commands. That was nothing new, he'd thought when given this information. When had she ever responded to requests or suggestions, never mind commands? But that was not laughable. He was as much to blame for her state as she was, leaving her as he had. Now there was no escape. He would be responsible for her until one or the other of them was dead.

Although he was alone in the house, Oliver made up his bed in his office and locked the door. He would not be able to sleep otherwise, but sleep was a long time coming. Over and over, the last days he spent in this house played in his mind, banishing all hope of precious oblivion.

He'd kept careful records of their bills—the usual rent, hydro, gas, and all the other costs of living, but it was the huge single payment he'd worked out with the debt counselor many years ago that was his main focus, debts to department stores, dress shops, credit cards, even furniture stores, although where the furniture ended up was anyone's guess. All of it amassed into one great debt he'd been chipping away at these long years. The promise to himself, that once the children and the debts were taken care of, kept him going, kept him alive. The day the last bill popped up on his computer screen, Oliver felt a charge of electricity shoot through him. He had expected it, calculated the exact day, time, and amount, but to see it on the screen in black and white—it was over. His debt was paid.

Since he'd left the Epperts and moved back into their home, Mona had been all but absent. Only once had she attempted to seduce him, but it was a half-hearted effort, walking into his office as she had, naked under her opened robe.

"Not a chance in hell," he said, a curl of disgust on his lip. She closed her dressing gown and tied the belt not with the expected rage at being rejected but like a tired-out hooker moving on to the next customer. A moment later, he felt sorry for her, but her come-on had been repulsive to him and far, far too late. His love for her had morphed into something other than desire. That a kernel of love for her had survived at all was a fact he had to bury under rational thought if he were to have a chance of freedom. He stayed for one more month in order to leave enough money for her to start anew and then one more to make sure his pension came through without a problem then he walked out the door a free man. That had been his plan, and that is exactly what played out except for Mona's final performance. How the gods must have laughed at him.

In the morning, he showered and shaved as he had in this house for almost thirty years, yet it seemed like he had been gone for ages. Only four days, but he'd covered so much ground. He wasn't afraid to look into the garage to see where Mona had nearly killed herself. He knew exactly where she'd done it.

His reasoning was to sever any connection he had to her act, as if that were possible. He stood drinking coffee on the back porch and looked out over the yard. Gone were all traces of his once gorgeous garden, replaced by grass that grew unevenly, interrupted here and there by patches of weeds. Since she'd destroyed it, Oliver had taken no more interest in the yard than to mow it every week or so. Mrs. White stepped into her yard to let her little dog out and looked over at him.

"Hello, Mrs. White. How are you after everything that has gone on?" he said as he stepped off the porch and walked to the fence. The dog ran up to greet Oliver, wiggling with all its might.

"It was a shock, Oliver. I'll say that. I've never seen anyone do such a thing. Why would she try to kill herself? You've had a terrible time of it all these years, but this…"

"I'm so sorry. The police told me what happened, how if it hadn't been for the postman and you, she would be gone." He said this trying to express gratitude, feeling anything but. "I'm going up to see her this morning to see what the prognosis is. Whatever happens, we'll be moving from here. I gave my notice to the university last month and they agreed to let Mona stay in the place for one more month until she found somewhere to live. Then this." Oliver reached down and scratched the dog's head before continuing. "You've been a good neighbor, and I have appreciated your friendship over the years, the kids, too. They asked after you. I came back almost as soon as I got off the train in Toronto. The kids live there and I was going to live there, too. Now, I'm not sure what will happen." He looked at the late-autumn chrysanthemums blooming profusely in Mrs. White's garden bordering the fence.

"The police asked me all kinds of questions, personal ones about you and your wife. I answered honestly. She was unhinged most of the time, I told them. But you, if it wasn't for you, those children would have had a terrible time of it. I told them that, too."

"Thank you, Mrs. White. I'm sure they appreciated your statement," he said, but he wondered how her words would be twisted by the police to put him in a worse light than the one in which he was. They needed a cause for every effect, and that cause had to be tangible. Mona's insanity was tangible to him and to his son and daughter, as tangible as a careening tank, but not to many others.

"I told them about the garden, too. They asked me how you reacted to that, did I hear any shouting or arguing. Not a sound, I said. You just came out and cleaned up the mess and that was an end to it."

Oliver smiled weakly at her and thanked her again before going back inside. She was right. He hadn't said a word to Mona about the yard. He had not spoken one word to her about the smashed jars of tomatoes, peaches, pears, and jam in the basement storeroom. After Gwen's departure, she'd destroyed every single jar he'd so carefully prepared, and left the mess for him to clean up, which he had done, of course. It wasn't his house. He would have to return it to the university in decent shape.

The university hospital was a far walk for Oliver, but the weather was cool and clear. He had time to unravel the confusion and disappointment in his mind and focus on what was right before him. He would formulate no plans until he spoke with Mona's doctors and until he saw what state she was in. Shirley's words came back to him. She'd described herself as a one-day-at-a-time kind of person—no planning ahead, no strategic moves to counteract an assault. Perhaps that was a freedom of sorts, taking life as it came, without anticipation. He'd had little practice at that approach, none, in fact, since Mona. Now he would focus on himself for a change, make decisions that would be good for him. But his interest in self-care plummeted the instant he walked into Mona's hospital room. He was unprepared for the sight of her to drive into him like a sucker punch to the gut.

Her slim body was contorted, and her hands pulled up into fists under her chin. He could not see her face because her head, twisted at a painful angle, bent too low. As ready as he had been for her attacks, nothing prepared him for the astonishing degree of emotion that sprung up in him as he saw her helpless form. What those emotions were took him some time to identify. Shock, of course, but pity as well. An undercurrent of anger propelled him to move closer. The anger of three decades filled him, but more terrible than that was his anger that she had not completed what she had begun, and now he would be responsible for her for the rest of her life. He felt as he had on the day she'd caused the car accident. How easy it would be to twist that dark and once-beautiful head of hers until her neck finally snapped ending her hold on him forever. She deserved the state she was in, but did he deserve to be burdened with her forever? Just one small twist and it would all be over.

Oliver broke down. In the ward with three other insentient patients, Oliver stood at the window beside Mona and let violent sobs shudder through his body. What had he become? What kind of man was he to push aside pity with such murderous thoughts? He had once been a good man, a kind man, and he had thought he could be that again if he could get over this hatred and this twisted love that poisoned his body and soul. He would have forgiven her in time if all he had to deal with were his thoughts and not her presence. But it was not she who needed forgiveness now. Who could forgive a man who had walked away from a woman he knew would harm herself? What kind of man could say to her, "Do your worst. I'm done," and not look back? What kind of man could then walk through the house, close the front door, and calmly speak to their neighbor about her garden and his trip as if nothing at all was happening? He was that man. And now he had his reward for such negligence, for such sins of inaction. He would never be free of her.

A hand rested on his shoulder. "Doctor Eastmund, I'm Doctor Curtis. I'm very sorry for your wife's condition. Perhaps we can go to my office to talk. I'll outline the extent of her debilities and help you with a plan for her care."

Oliver wiped his hand across his face and nodded, unable to utter a word. He followed the doctor out of the room and down several halls, finally reaching the office. It was a large, light-filled room, sparse and neat. The doctor searched for a file as he sat behind his desk. Oliver took a chair across from him.

Doctor Curtis looked into Oliver's face before he turned the screen toward him. "Are you able to hear the details at this point? Is there someone you would like to have with you?" He had a kind face, open and compassionate. A tinge of sadness pulled at the corners of his eyes.

Oliver nodded, cleared his throat, and said, "Yes, the details are important. My children are in Toronto, and they are the only ones I would like here, but that is not possible. I'll pass along the information to them. Please go ahead."

"In some respects," the doctor began, "your wife was lucky." He opened the folder and a diagram of blood vessels running through a head and neck appeared. "She didn't fall from a great height, so her neck did not break. However," he said, pointing to the diagram, "she has experienced brain ischemia. What that means is, because of strangulation, all the veins and arteries carrying blood to and from her brain were blocked, preventing oxygen from getting through. We cannot survive more than ten minutes without an oxygen supply to the brain. It's not an exact rule, but the longer the brain goes without oxygen, the more far-reaching and permanent the damage. Apparently, someone must have performed CPR quite quickly or not enough oxygen would have traveled to the brain for her to have survived at all."

Flatly, Oliver said, "The postman. And my neighbor. Mrs. White. They performed CPR. They saved Mona's life." He had them to thank for saving Mona, one a woman she hated and who in turn disliked her. And it all must have happened within minutes of him leaving and riding the train, not once conceiving that she would be rescued from herself and that he would be damned in a way that had not arisen in his worst nightmare. On the train, he played the role of a soon-to-be ex-spouse. Made phone calls to a phantom. Preparing the stage for his next act as a widower, only to have her resurrected and clinging to him, pulling him down with her forever. Saving her from death had been his role in the past. But he was no Orpheus. Her death was to have been his life.

"The important thing for you to understand, Doctor Eastmund, is that this damage is permanent. She will not recover. She will most likely have a shortened lifespan, how short is an unknown. She will need constant and continuous care in an institution."

"There is no way for me to care for her at home?" Oliver asked, his disingenuousness obvious to him alone.

"It is possible, but she would need nurses present day and night. It's not a recommended option. Most medical plans will not cover that, and it is prohibitively expensive."

"I'm moving to Toronto. Can I have her transferred to an institution there?"

"If there's room. We'll have to call ahead and find out what's available, but a social worker will help you with the details."

On the walk home, Oliver tried to sort out all of the information the doctor and social worker had given him. Mona would remain in the university hospital until a place could be found either in Vancouver or Toronto. He would simply have to wait until word came back. That night, he called Gavin and gave him the news.

"She won't be moving here, in our…your place," Gavin said. Oliver heard the relief in his voice.

"No, I can't afford round-the-clock nursing. She will be placed in a care facility either here or somewhere in the Toronto area. When I have more facts, I'll call. Will you tell Gwen? I've got a pile of work to do in the house to get rid of stuff and clean it up before the end of the month. If there is anything you'd like from the place, tell me. I plan on either throwing or giving everything away."

"No, Dad. Do what you feel best. I need nothing from that house. I'll check with Gwen, but I'm sure she feels the same. She didn't have time to tell you, but she's been seeing someone pretty regularly. She kept him to herself until they'd been going out for about six months. He seems like a good guy. Dillon. His name's Dillon McCarthy. He's a doctor at the psychiatric hospital where Gwen is doing her practicum. It could be serious. But I'll let her tell you all about him. With Gwen and Dillon working on it, I am sure a place can be found here for Mona if that's your choice. When will you be back?"

"It all depends upon what can be found for your mother."

"Don't call her that," Gavin said sharply. "I haven't thought of her as my mother for a long time. Just call her Mona."

Oliver paused to take in Gavin's tone. "Okay, son," he said. *Careful.* He would not correct Gavin, a grown man entitled to his feelings. He worried, though, that Gavin would be the worse off for such hatred. God knows *he* was. "Everything has to be out of the house in two weeks, so I hope to be in Toronto after I've finished here regardless of where your...Mona ends up."

In the morning, after a second cup of coffee, Oliver opened the door to Mona's room. He hadn't been in there since she'd destroyed the garden. Four years of trash, dirty clothes, and discarded food. Four years without vacuuming or dusting or scrubbing the bathroom. How had she lived like this? How had she managed not to contract some disease? The smell alone made Oliver's stomach heave. Rather than do laundry, she had purchased new clothes. That much was obvious from the number of bags and clothing tags scattered everywhere. A huge pile of laundry occupied one corner. The condition of the room made his decision easy—everything must go. All of it thrown out, the dirty plates and glasses, plastic cutlery and food packaging. This is what she spent her money on, this and going out most days and evenings. At least, she had never brought anyone home with her. Oliver was grateful for that, held he would not have put up with it.

He was also grateful that Mona had remained strangely silent after her destruction of the garden and his return from Felix Eppert's home. Perhaps it was because she was convinced she'd completely demoralized him. After she'd destroyed the garden and he'd cleaned up the yard and basement, escaped for those few days and came back, the only thing he'd said to her was his oft-repeat threat. "Now that the kids are gone, as soon as our debts are paid, I will leave you." It was a truth that may have finally sunk in. No matter what the cause, she'd left him mercifully alone for the most part until he'd fulfilled his threat.

He chose a few items from her room that he thought she might need wherever she ended up, things like casual pants and shirts, sweaters, socks and underwear, and two nightgowns. A housecoat and slippers and a pair of slip-on flat shoes. These he would wash and pack for her. He would buy a new toothbrush and other toiletries. Everything else was either too filthy or damaged to keep.

He had not expected any of himself, but he was saddened that she had not one picture of the children in her room. He found ripped photos of Hewitt and a few other strangers, men, as he tore through the trash. By the time he was finished with Mona's room, there were thirty huge orange bags of garbage ready for pick up the next morning. He called a service to remove the mattresses and would give the furniture and other household goods to whatever thrift store would come by to get them. In three days, the place was almost empty, and he could begin cleaning and repairing the scrapes, dents and holes in the walls made by pictures and mirrors and other hanging or thrown things. Most of these items had been sold by Mona over the years, but the evidence of what had been there remained. It was a disheartening task that made Oliver feel he was wading through chest-high muck trying to reach solid ground. This home had deserved much better than the family who'd lived here. Both the house and the children had deserved so much more. He would get this job done by putting one foot in front of the other. Step by weary step, he thought of his task as inching his way toward a precarious detachment.

When at last the house was empty and the keys returned to the plant manager at the university, Oliver booked himself into a hotel. He was there only two nights when the social worker called to say they had a place for Mona in Toronto and would fly her there in a week. His plan would cover some of the costs, but he would have to come up with the rest. It was right that the medical system should pay since it was the system that had refused to help her and them while she wielded her insanity. And he would pay his part since it was a small price to cover his guilt.

The following morning, he went to the hospital with a suitcase full of Mona's clean clothes. She was in bed, arms bent and hands curled beneath her chin, her legs drawn up. He could hardly see her face for her hair. He brushed it back. Her eyes were closed and did not open when he called her name. As he pulled the blankets up to her chin, a nurse came in and smiled at him.

"She's holding her own," she said.

"That's the best we can hope for. I've been told she will be moved to Toronto next week. I expect they will call me when she gets to the nursing home."

"I'm not sure of the procedure, but I imagine her caseworker will have all the information. Does she have other family there?"

Oliver looked at the young nurse who seemed genuinely concerned about her patient. "Yes," he said, his words covering up an enormity of pain and struggle. "Our daughter and her fiancé made the arrangements. Our son and his wife also live there. We'll soon be grandparents."

"That will be nice," she offered.

What else could she say? Too bad your wife won't know what the hell is going on? Too bad that grandchild will be better off without one grandmother? Too bad she'd made so many people's lives miserable enough that they'd wished her dead?

He smiled at the nurse and sighed. When she left, he gathered his backpack and suitcase and headed for the airport. He would be in Toronto before nightfall.

Chapter 22

"Open your eyes," Theresa said, sounding like a child on Christmas morning.

Oliver stood still, astonished at the bright new openness of the living room and kitchen of the renovated coach house.

"There's more." Theresa's excitement added to the glow of the room. "Here's the bathroom, and the laundry room is right beside it. Wait until you see the bedrooms."

"Take it easy, Theresa. Let Dad catch his breath." Gavin put his arm around his wife and gave her a hug.

Gwendolyn was just as animated. "I helped with the decorating. You have everything you need. Look, a coffee maker. It's an espresso machine."

Oliver couldn't speak. For a man who had been waging war all of his life, he was toppled by the kindness and generosity of his children. "You did too much. This is too much, far too much."

"You deserve this and more, Dad," Gavin said, suddenly serious. "You took care of us, now it's our turn to take care of you. You have complete independence here, and can come and go as you please. There's a patio out back beyond the dining room, and two bedrooms and a bath upstairs. There's a little balcony off the master bedroom so you can have coffee with the birds in the morning."

"Gavin, Theresa. I have no words. Gwen, I can't believe what I'm seeing." He reached out for his daughter and put his arm around her shoulders. It was a stunning house, half the coach house. The soft blue-gray walls framed by crisp white molding and baseboards, tall windows along the front and back. The furniture was comfortable and stylish, and the bookshelves were already stacked with the volumes he had sent ahead. The floors like bleached wood shone clean and bright. Beds, dressers and night stands occupied the bedrooms, and the linen closet was stocked with extra towels and bedding. A bowl of fruit sat on the kitchen counter, and when Gavin opened the fridge, all the staples Oliver could need filled the shelves as they did the cupboards.

"You even have dishes, pots and pans, cutlery, everything you need." Gwen put her arm around him and leaned her head on his shoulder. "I knew you'd like it," she said.

"We'll let you get the feel of the place. You must be exhausted. Dinner is at eight tonight, so whenever you are ready, come up to the house," Theresa said as she led Gavin to the door. "But don't get used to having dinner cooked for you every night. Tonight's special," Theresa warned, and they laughed with her.

Tired, full, and happy, Oliver returned to his…he wasn't sure what to call it. It was his home. It wasn't an apartment. It was certainly much more than that. A townhouse? The coach house. That was the only thing he could call it. He searched for the light switch. Soon it would be automatic—his reach for lights, doors, rooms, but for now, he drew joy from the newness of it all. How could he be so lucky? His children had grown up to be generous and kind people of whom he was proud. Undeserving as he felt, to disturb a thing in the pristine kitchen seemed like it would be a desecration. Even taking a shower seemed invasive. But after such a long day, a long and difficult life, a washing-off of the old Oliver Eastmund was necessary in order to make way for the new Oliver Rook.

Just before climbing into bed, Oliver searched through his wallet and found Shirley's card. He called her number. He had to share his great fortune with someone, and who better than the woman who had helped him struggle toward freedom on that train. He wanted her to know that everything had worked out well.

She answered on the first ring. "Hello traveling buddy. How is life treating you these days?"

"At the moment, life is good, great, in fact. How about you?"

"I'm going to be in Toronto day after tomorrow, and I was wondering if you'd like to get together for a coffee before I head back to Vancouver."

Why not, thought Oliver. *Why not invite her here?* She would be his first guest, and it would be good to see her. She agreed.

Oliver slept that night like he had not slept in years. He slept with the bedroom door open, the window open. He slept until the light of dawn woke him. He slept as if he were free and innocent, without a care in the world. He made coffee in a machine he was not sure of, finally figuring out how to slot the pod into the right place. Never had coffee tasted so good. He stepped out onto his patio that looked across the large back garden. Gavin, Theresa, and Gwen had thought of everything—the blue mosaic of the table matched the garden planters, and the umbrella was tilted to shade him from the rising sun. A distant hum of traffic and the songs of autumn's few remaining birds were the only sounds. The main house was far enough away that he could hear nothing coming from that quarter although someday soon, he hoped to hear the sounds of his grandchild, perhaps grandchildren, their laughter and exuberance.

He heard a car door close and its engine come to life. Gavin was leaving for the office. No wonder he was doing so well. He'd be there before eight in the morning and be home well after six. This is what Theresa had told him during dinner last night.

"He loves his job, Dad. I am sure when the baby comes, he'll adjust his hours." Theresa had said this as she gave Gavin a look that said he'd best agree. Gavin said nothing, but he looked at her with all the affection in the world. He couldn't wait to be a father.

Oliver thought about Gwen's doctor, Dillon McCarthy. He'd arrived just in time for dinner last night. He seemed a kind, if quiet, man, dark-haired, stocky. He was as tall as Gwen, and he clearly cared for her. Even though he was a psychiatrist, thankfully, they avoided any discussion of Mona, her condition both past and present. Oliver's greatest joy was for Gwen to be happy, and he found no fault with Dillon at this point, but he was not the best judge of character.

The first full day in his new home, Oliver examined the garden, noted the strategic placement of plants for the best appreciation of their blooming times. Rudbeckia, chrysanthemums, and rosy sedum filled the garden with autumn colors. There were no vegetable beds, but then again, anyone who could afford the kind of house Gavin and Theresa had didn't need to grow their own vegetables. Perhaps he could convince them to give him a little plot of land in which to grow a few tomatoes, carrots, and onions.

He slept well the second night, filled with gratitude for his unbelievable good fortune. In the morning, as Oliver sipped his second cup of coffee, his phone rang.

"Doctor Eastmund?" the voice at the other end asked.

"Yes, or I should say this is the former Mr. Eastmund now Rook, Oliver Rook."

"Are you the husband of Mona Eastmund?" The voice sounded a little more panicked now.

"Yes?" He said it as a question. What now?

"Mr. Eastmund, or Rook, your wife has arrived at the Toronto airport, but there has been a mix up. The residence where she was to go doesn't have room for her at the moment. We've contacted the hospital in Vancouver, but she cannot go back there either. We will get this straightened out, but it may take a few days or a week or so. Can she stay with you? We can provide nursing care around the clock, but there simply isn't room for her in her assigned residence."

Oliver froze. Of course, it was all too good to be true. Mona's grasp on his life would never end. He could not speak. He would make sure she was cared for properly in a nursing home, but that was it. A single picture of Mona in his uncontaminated home was more repulsive to him than his lifetime of memories of her.

"Mr. Rook, are you there?"

He could hang up. He should just hang up. They did not have his address, but they would be able to find him, eventually. He'd have to change his driver's license and his medical card. But by then, they would have taken care of the problem. Of Mona.

"Yes, I'm here. How could you make such a mistake with people's lives?"

"I understand your frustration, Mr. Rook, but—"

"No, you have no idea of my frustration. You haven't a clue."

"Mr. Rook, if you just give me your address, we will bring your wife to you along with nurses. Are you able to accommodate them?"

"If I said no, what would you do?"

"She would likely end up in the hallway of one of the overcrowded hospitals without proper care and attention. Is that what you want?"

"What I want is for you people to do your jobs." He could say no more. He knew he was defeated the moment the caller asked if he had room for Mona. Of course, he did. He had a spare room. He could even put a bed in the living room and have one nurse in the spare room, but that is not what he wanted. When, however, had anyone other than his children cared about his wants or needs? He gave the woman his address. He had told Mona he would leave her when the children were gone and the debts paid, a caution so that she should prepare herself for such a day, he'd told himself. In spite of how often he'd resigned himself to her control over his life, he had not prepared himself for the forever burden of her. The hope of freedom had kept him going. She would be here in about two hours.

"I'm sorry, Theresa. This is not what any of us would choose, but the residence screwed-up. I just hope Gavin isn't too upset."

"You and me both," Theresa said.

He was more than upset. Theresa called him before he left for home. Mona was ensconced in a bed made up in the living room, and the promised nurse had gone out to get some needed supplies. Oliver heard Gavin's car pull into the driveway. He winced as the car door slammed. Gavin went straight to the house. Oliver heard that door slam as well. He worried for Theresa, but he knew Gavin was not a violent man. Theresa was capable and strong enough to keep him in check, but she shouldn't have to. This was Oliver's fault, not hers. Even when the nurse came back, Gavin did not come to the coach house. Oliver made a simple pasta dinner for himself and the nurse who had offered to do the cooking. He looked over at Mona from time to time, but he was not equipped to see to her needs. He helped adjust her when the nurse raised her bed to a semi-upright position, but other than that, he remained useless. In true Oliver fashion, he found himself grateful that Mona could no longer scream at him or throw a tantrum, but then he felt the familiar guilt at such uncharitable thoughts.

That night was a long, sleepless one. Once again, Oliver felt trapped in his room, the door closed. He was unwilling to go downstairs in the dark where Mona lay in her near-vegetative state. The coach house would forever be tainted by her presence regardless of her silence. He heard the night nurse fussing around the place, checking on Mona and making herself at home. At six, he got up as the nurse again saw to her patient before the day nurse arrived. He made coffee for both of them and went out on the patio. It was chilly, too cool to sit in his robe, but it was better than being inside watching Mona and the administrations of the nurse.

Before long, he heard the house door slam. Then voices. Loud angry voices.

"You don't have to take it out on me, Gavin. Get a grip!"

Oliver had never heard Theresa so angry.

Gavin answered back in a quieter but more enraged voice. "You should have said no. What would they have done, left her on the runway? They would have found something."

Oliver walked around the coach house to the driveway. "Gavin, it's my fault, not Theresa's. I'm sorry, son. I'm the one who should have said no. It's me you should be angry with."

"I'm that as well," Gavin answered. "Why the hell did you let her come here? This is *MY* home! *MY* life! I moved across the country to get away from her, and you bring her here. What the hell were you thinking?"

"Son, I know—"

"No, you don't know!" Gavin's voice was hoarse from shouting, but he continued, "You have no idea what it was like growing up in that house with her. You did a good job of protecting us, but you have no idea of the gut-wrenching existence Gwen and I had." Gavin paused. Theresa moved toward him, her hand outstretched, but Gavin shrugged her away.

"I went to bed at night planning where to hide if she came in my room and tried to kill me. A little kid, and I thought my own *mother* would kill me. You want to hear what my pathetic little plan was? To hide between my mattress and box spring. That's how insignificant I felt. I thought no one would find me there. I never tried it. If it wasn't possible, where else could I go? So I kept it just to ease my mind. But I did tell Gwen. You see, I had to protect her, too, from our murderous *mother*, Gwen and you. What would happen if you died, too, like Grandma?"

Oliver, paralyzed by Gavin's upsurge of emotion, uttered, "Oh, Gavin. I didn't know—"

"No, you didn't. I couldn't tell you. I couldn't add to what you were already carrying. But I told Gwen, and she tried it. She tried to get between her mattress and box spring, but she couldn't do it. She wasn't strong enough, so I told her if Mona broke into her room to hide in the very back of her closet." He sobbed, "But then it dawned on me that she would be trapped there with no way out, but I didn't have another plan except to stay awake and listen. I hid a knife, a big kitchen knife far under my mattress, far enough so you wouldn't find it when you changed the bedding, and I stayed awake as long as I could. If she came after me, I'd be okay. If she came after Gwen, I would grab the knife and go in after her.

"Here's another thing you didn't have a clue about," he added, spiteful in his anger. "Gwen told me that she wouldn't make a sound if Mona came to attack her. She wouldn't make a sound because she did not want me to kill our *mother*." He spat the word. "Not for Mona's sake but because she was trying to keep me or you from getting into trouble for killing her. That's how we tried to take care of each other, so don't tell me you know. You have no idea what our lives were like."

Gavin took in great angry gulps of air. He glared at Oliver, daring him to say something, daring him to try to lessen the toxic rage he spewed out like a volcanic surge.

"Do you remember when you told me to apologize to her for calling her a slut? I never told you what she said to me because it would have hurt you."

"Gavin, don't. You don't have to do this," Theresa pleaded.

"*He* didn't have to do *this*!" Gavin shouted, waving his hand toward the coach house, toward Mona. The nurse opened the door to see what was causing such an uproar.

"I'll tell you what she said." Gavin's voice was again restrained and enraged. "She told me that I was a weakling, a weak man just like you. That I'd never amount to anything." He all but sobbed. "She said that I'd never find a girlfriend much less a wife, and if I did, she'd run around on me just like Mona did to you because I wasn't a man, not a real man."

Theresa broke in. "Gavin, please," she cried.

But he couldn't stop. His shoulders heaved as he struggled to keep from losing control. "She said she was a slut because you, you..." he pointed at Oliver, "were useless, and I...she said I was as useless as you. Do you have any idea what it was like to be a teenager with his own *mother* saying this about him, about his father? It was hell fighting her words every day of my life, proving her wrong about both of us. It was pure hell not to see you as she saw you. I had to work so hard not to hate you the way I hated her, not because I believed her but because you didn't take us and run."

A loud strangulated croak came from the open door of the coach house. Mona was laughing. At him. At Gavin. He was sure of it, but how was it possible? The nurse turned back to her patient. For all she knew, it was a poor damaged woman choking. But Oliver knew better.

Pain shot from Oliver's neck down his arm. It hit his chest with such force that he fell to his knees. "Son," he managed to breathe out hoarsely as a weight like that of an anvil crushed his chest. He struggled to take a breath, reaching for Gavin. Both Theresa and Gavin ran to him. Oliver's eyes shifted past Gavin. Shirley, an old woman, was stumbling quickly and falteringly toward them as the blackness of unconsciousness enfolded him.

Chapter 23

The bright afternoon sun warmed the room and woke Oliver. Before he opened his eyes, he listened to the sounds feathering the edges of consciousness. Like a rake over gravel, Shirley's voice announced her presence. Gavin was there, too. Oliver heard him clear his throat. Someone stood up, for Oliver heard a chair scrape the floor, a sound that would forever tear at his soul. Footsteps.

"Hello," Gavin said.

"Are you family?" the newcomer to the room asked.

"Yes. I'm his son, Gavin, and this is Shirley, a good friend. Are you his doctor?"

"Yes, Gill Rajan. I'm your father's cardiologist. Has he spoken to you yet?"

"No," Gavin said. "He hasn't woken up. Should we be worried?"

"Not at all. He's been through a lot. Sleep is the best thing for him right now."

Oliver listened. They would likely say more, tell the truth, if they thought he wasn't able to hear.

"Is there much damage to the heart?" Shirley asked.

"No, not that we can see. He will have to take it easy for a while, watch his diet, avoid stress. Don't wake him. I'll come back later." Oliver heard the doctor's soft steps as he left the room.

Gavin said, "Avoid stress—that's a joke. Not with Mona around. Thanks, by the way, for getting her into the residence so quickly. What was it you do again?"

"Chair of the Provincial Health Services Authority in British Columbia. Former chair, I should say. I gave it up some years ago when I turned seventy-five. I got to know a person or two in my time. Having your mother in care should give your dad some relief."

Oliver could picture Gavin recoiling from the word mother, and Shirley must have as well.

"You don't like your mother much, do you?" she asked.

Gavin snorted at the understatement. "You could say that. She made our lives hell. My dad did his best to protect us when we were kids, but she was a monster. She wasn't supposed to come anywhere near my home."

"Yes, I heard. I was coming up the drive when you were giving your dad a piece of your mind."

Gavin said nothing. Oliver knew his look of shame mingled with resentment, could clearly picture it.

"I'm not family, and I have no right to butt in, but I'm an old woman, so I've learned a thing or three over the years. One of those things is that we only get to know ourselves in relation to others. You've picked up some pretty good skills watching your dad maneuver through life, but you've also come to see things in yourself by being in a relationship with the rest of your family, your mother, too."

"Don't call her that. She's Mona to me."

"Okay, Mona," Shirley said as gently as her rough voice allowed. "You've learned something about yourself because of Mona. Can you put your finger on it?"

"That I hate her for what she's done to all of us." Gavin sounded like a petulant child rather than the brilliant lawyer he was.

"Turn that around, and you can see that what she has done to you has made you very protective of your home, your family. Anything else?"

Oliver listened. The seconds took an eternity. Gavin cleared he throat. He could tell Shirley to mind her own business. But as he'd learned on the train, Shirley seemed to draw a person out of himself. But not this time. Gavin was sure to have clamped his jaws, his eyes piercing. He hoped that glare was not directed at Shirley, but she could handle herself.

"I used to get angry a lot and at the wrong people," Shirley said. "Too often. Usually at the people in my life who didn't deserve it. My husband was a brutal man, but I couldn't confront him for a number of reasons, mostly because I knew he would never change and I couldn't handle the backlash, so I misdirected that anger for a long time."

Gavin jumped in. "I have a right to be angry, don't I?"

"I don't know. Maybe you do. I'm not the judge. But now that you've come face to face with a less-than-admirable characteristic, you can do something about it. You can't do anything about the things you refuse to recognize. You can change those things you do see about yourself and don't like. The question is, what are you going to do about your anger?"

"What did you do with yours?" Gavin asked. He sounded less aggressive, less defensive.

"Well, first of all, I left. Then I got a divorce. But I was still angry. Finally, I recognized that that anger was passion disguised as something negative. I was passionate about people being treated fairly, so I put that passion to good use. I was a nurse, but I became a patient advocate. Then I moved up the line to positions where I could wield changes more far-reaching."

Shirley continued. "I haven't had the chance to really get to know your sister Gwendolyn very well, but it seems that through her profession, she chose to try to figure out what made Mona tic. Daily, she plunges herself into facing Mona's madness, or at least those with madness like hers. Every day she interacts with psychosis. Whether she was conscious of it or not, she likely recognized that she didn't grasp why Mona behaved as she did, so she took charge, faced the daemon, and learned—not so much because she thought she could change her mother, but likely because she decided not to live in fear—not to blame anyone or anything except Mona's mental illness. Now, I'm just guessing at this, given the facts. You know your sister better than I, but with knowledge comes power. Same with you. With knowledge about your anger, comes the power to change, redirect."

Whether she was aware he was listening or not, Oliver, too, recognized the truth when he heard it. Anger, yes. But it was guilt that he'd had to live with. What was guilt? How could he turn that around? He was so focused on the changes he would have to make that he forgot he was feigning sleep. He coughed.

"Hello there. Have a good sleep?" Shirley said.

"Welcome to the land of the living. You gave us a scare," added Gavin.

Before Oliver could respond, Shirley looked up toward the door, and Gavin turned in his seat then stood and greeted the heavy-set doctor who walked into the room.

"Hello Doctor Rook. I'm Gill Rajan, your cardiologist. How are you feeling?"

"Like I've been on the losing end of a train wreck. At least the pain is gone. I'm just very tired. And it's Oliver. You can drop the doctor. How long have I been here? What's happened to Mona? Where is she?"

"Don't worry, Dad. She's been taken care of. She's in good hands. We'll tell you all about it later. For now," Gavin said, "let's concentrate on you."

He had been in the hospital for a little over a day and a half and would stay for another three or four days, just to be sure, but no surgery was required. He'd had a blood-vessel spasm that temporarily blocked the blood flow to his heart. He'd have to get some regular exercise, watch the fat and carb intake, and practice meditation or learn some other way to calm himself. He could stand to lose a little weight, but otherwise, he should be fine. When the doctor left, Shirley, too, announced her departure.

"I've got to get to the station. Time to go back to Vancouver. You're in good hands here." Shirley put her hand on Gavin's back, and he opened his arms and gave her the hug Oliver wished he could also give. Shirley bent down and kissed Oliver on the forehead. "You get better and take care of yourself. I've got to have someone to visit on the long waits between trains."

After she left, Gavin sat down and filled him in on the missing details.

"Your friend Shirley pulled a few strings and got Mona into the care home almost immediately after your collapse."

"How'd she do that?" Oliver asked as if he hadn't heard their earlier exchange. He'd been so focused on his own problems on the train trip that seemed a lifetime ago that he hadn't asked Shirley much about herself. He barely knew her, yet she'd jumped right into the ugliness of his life.

Gavin filled him in. "Apparently," he said, "she's got connections with people who can get things done. She took charge right away, first looking after you and then getting Theresa settled as well, once she saw that Theresa was pregnant. Then she got the gears in motion to move Mona. She's a powerful force." Gavin said this without looking in Oliver's eyes. He spoke to Oliver's hands that were folded across his stomach over the blankets.

"I forgot I'd invited Shirley for coffee," Oliver said.

Gavin sat by the bed clasping his hands between his knees. "Look, Dad," he began.

"Don't worry about it, son. You were right to be angry. I was wrong to spring things on you the way I did." Oliver had no need of an apology. He did not deserve one. He'd brought this on himself, and there was no one else to blame.

"I shouldn't have lost it the way I did."

"I know, Son. I know." How could he explain to Gavin that no matter how hard he tried to get away from her, she'd always be a part of him. He had her eyes, both he and Gwendolyn. They both had her stunning good looks. At least Gavin didn't have Oliver's cowardice, his weakness. He did not have a molecule of Oliver in him. He was more resilient than that. "I'm sorry to have put you in such a position."

Gavin said nothing. He reached over and clutched Oliver's hand in an awkward grip, and the two of them remained that way until a nurse came into the room.

The coach house was back to its original configuration—Mona's hospital bed was gone, and so was all the paraphernalia the nurse had brought. Not a trace was left. Oliver took it easy for a week or so, going on short walks around the neighborhood, venturing further and further each day. Winter was closing in, and soon snow would impede his outings. He studied bus routes and subway lines, memorized directions to bookstores and to Gwendolyn's university and her new home. She and Dillon were planning a spring wedding—nothing elaborate. Gwen disliked showy affairs, and Dillon simply wanted Gwendolyn. He was a good man. He'd come on his own to see Oliver in the hospital and had given him some much-needed advice.

"People who've lived a long time with those who have the kind of mental illness I suspect Mona had often need some emotional and psychological help. Many—and I'm not diagnosing you, just offering an expert opinion—suffer from post-traumatic stress disorder or PTSD. I'm sure you've heard of it. I can give you the names of a few people in that field."

Oliver took him up on his offer and made an appointment for himself for early in the new year, at a time when he hoped his physical well-being would be optimal. Throughout their upbringing, he had taken the children to see counselors, but he had insisted the focus be on them, their welfare in the face of Mona's craziness. They had been exposed to normal families, intact families, through their friends, and such influence had been invaluable. Now it was his turn. He would, for the sake of his children and his future grandchild, try, with a therapist's help, not to drag the festered past into their present lives. The simple act of making that decision eased his mind and made him feel as if he had taken a huge step forward.

On an unusually warm morning, Oliver sat out on his patio. Sheltered and sunny, it seemed more like summer than late autumn. He was used to such days on the West Coast, but it was an unexpected gift in Toronto, From the sounds of it, several neighbors were also enjoying the reprieve. Oliver heard voices in the driveway, but he assumed it was Gavin speaking with the landscaper about winterizing the gardens. Lighter work like pruning the rose bushes and shoring them up with leaves was something he could do, and he hoped he'd have the opportunity. The steady crunch of gravel underfoot caught Oliver's attention, and he looked up to see his brother Derek walking toward him.

"What the hell are you doing here?" Oliver said as he stood and embraced his brother.

"You didn't have to go through all this trouble to get my attention," Derek replied. "Gavin got hold of me and told me what's happened. He says you're doing okay now. Is that right?"

"Yeah, I'm fine, just fine. No harm done, just some kind of blood vessel spasm. I'm okay. But you…" Oliver held his brother by his shoulders and pushed him an arm's length back. "You look like an ad for suntan lotion. What have you been up to?"

"Oh, you know, a little of this and that. I've got my own line of waterboards—surf, skim, paddle—snowboards, too. I'm headquartered out of Tofino now. Just moved up from L.A. after all the political shit down there. Thought it was time to get back home. I just do administration now. I've got some good kids working for me, so I can take time off. I was about to call when Gavin called and filled me in. Mona's in a home? She gonna make it?"

Oliver, aware that Derek asked after Mona without a disparaging comment, looked down at his coffee. "Not for long. She's pretty much finished. Can't talk, can't move on her own. I don't know how they get her to eat. I usually go up after lunch. You can come with me, if you like."

Derek declined as Oliver knew he would. No love was lost between him and Mona. He'd hated her after her attempt at seducing him. He'd come to visit them about a month after their wedding, and on his first night there, Mona came into his bedroom. She'd laughed even as he turned her around and shoved her out the door, putting a chair under the doorknob. When he'd told Oliver, Derek had tried his best to be kind, but he'd told him to get rid of her. Leave her. She was nothing but trouble. But Oliver was sure Derek had misinterpreted Mona's intentions, sure she was just trying to see that he had everything he needed. And then she'd announced her pregnancy. What was he to do? The brothers had been in contact sporadically after that. Derek avoided Mona, ignored her whenever they accidentally met. He'd get together with Oliver and the children from time to time at Jericho Beach or English Bay in Vancouver, but he'd never come to the house again. Gwendolyn and Gavin, however, had remained in touch with their uncle even after they'd moved away from home.

It was good to see Derek. He looked healthy, happy. Although he was two years younger than Oliver, he looked more like ten years his junior. Derek stood a good four inches taller than Oliver. They were both dark-haired and sturdily built, but the outdoor life had benefited Derek in ways with which the academic life could not compete. More likely it was the Mona effect that had worn Oliver down, but whatever the cause, Derek brought with him some much-needed positive energy.

The brothers sat in the sunshine and caught up, reminiscing about childhood, their parents, but mostly about Derek's unorthodox life. He'd had ups and downs, a few bankruptcies.

"Once, in Australia, I slept rough for two months after I lost my surfing sponsorship from a major sporting-goods company. Apparently, a girl I was friendly with was the CEO's daughter, and she was supposed to go back to university. Unfortunately for him, I invited her to stay on the circuit. In the end, I lost the backing and the girl. Such is life." Derek regaled him and Gavin, who'd joined them, with tales like this from his past. The three laughed so hard that Theresa came out to see what she was missing.

"You've never settled down? Never thought about a home, family?" asked Oliver.

"No, never," Derek said. "Didn't do much for you, did it? Except the kids, of course." An awkward moment passed. He looked over to Gavin and Theresa. "I'm looking forward to being a great uncle, though," and the conversation turned to the baby.

Oliver made lunch for all of them before announcing his departure to visit Mona.

"You go on," Derek said. "I'll be here for a little over a week. Time enough to catch up."

The trip to reach the care home where Mona had been sent took Oliver about half an hour. As the subway rushed him underground, he thought about how Shirley had taken care of so much while he was laid up. She was a good friend. Someone he could count on, and someone who asked nothing of him except his friendship. His feelings were the same toward her, except he was in her debt. He'd be there in a minute if Shirley needed help, grateful as he was to live alone and in peace in the coach house near his children. And now with his brother in contact once again, Oliver breathed deeply and sat up straighter, his shoulders lightened. He looked around the nearly-full subway car. Almost all the passengers had their faces in their phones, isolating themselves from those around them. He wondered what kind of lives they lived. Did they have problems? Were they worse than his? And where were they going, these strangers moving together in self-imposed separateness? To work or to shop? Were they going to visit family or friends who were ill? Maybe some were going to attend funerals or celebrations of life. Each one of them had a story of loss or joy, or perhaps they simply plodded along in mundane repetition avoiding the highs and lows, keeping an even keel. He would have settled for that—routine, humdrum, dull. He would have been grateful for monotony.

His plan was to visit Mona twice a week for the first month or so. He made his way by bus and then subway to the Darlene Brisa Care Home. Eventually, the trip would become part of his daily outing. He chose to visit in the afternoons, after the ordeal of lunch was over, and read to her from the classics—Jane Austen, the Brontës, Defoe, Hardy. He would read her the poetry of Rilke and Blake, Dorothy Parker and Gerard Manley Hopkins whose poem *Spring and Fall* always touched him no matter how many times he read it. In the autumn of his life, it was a poem that reminded him of just how much he had become inured to, unconscious of. With everything he had, he pushed to rekindle his appreciation for life, for the simple pleasures that he'd missed for so long. The slant of light through trees, moving water, leaf stains on the sidewalks, the first snow of the season. A simple walk along a tree-lined city street began to give him the reverberations of the joy that had been repressed for so long. He had settled for the infrequent quiet times during which he'd managed to hold Mona's tantrums at bay, grateful for her silence. Now, her silence was all but assured, and his energy could be put to other uses like love, family, home—all things he had worked so hard to attain but was never able to enjoy. Yet he carried his burden of guilt. He was not an innocent bystander in Mona's decline.

This afternoon, Oliver was satisfied to sit with Mona, and he opened a book of poetry. Choosing a verse at random, he read aloud:

Had I the heavens' embroidered cloths,
Enwrought with golden and silver light,
The blue and the dim and the dark cloths
Of night and light and the half-light,
I would spread the cloths under your feet:
But I, being poor, have only my dreams;
Tread softly because you tread on my dreams.

Oliver knew the poem well. It was one he'd first learned in high school and was part of one by Yeats he'd taught over the years. Sitting beside Mona's twisted form, her arms and legs contracted and rigid, her neck as severely twisted as it had been the first time he'd seen her after she'd tried to hang herself, Oliver practiced the deep breathing he'd learned to try to quiet his anxiety. All along, his dreams had been profoundly trampled by Mona's madness, but at once it hit him fully and overpoweringly that her dreams, too, had been trod over by life, by her madness, even by him. He was not the man she wanted or needed. He could not be that for her. No one could.

Everyone, no matter where in life they stood—a Harvard University professor or alcoholic in a New York City drunk tank—started out with hopes and dreams to accomplish and to shine. But Oliver had not built his dreams around Mona, not since the children. He had focused his life and love on Gavin and Gwendolyn, and now on Theresa and the soon-to-be grandchild. He'd had to keep Mona foremost in his mind simply to defend himself and others against her, but his aspirations did not embrace her. Perhaps the only way she knew to keep herself present was to be as malicious as she could, evil and unforgettable. He'd distanced himself from loving her after she'd lashed out the first few times. He'd pulled back his affection further when the children came along. It seemed the only way to save them and himself. And her near-death. That, too, had destroyed any chance of her living whatever dreams she may have had. That he had no idea what her dreams may have been surprised him with a further twist of guilt. She was foremost in his mind at this moment, out of remorse.

"Pulchritude," he said softly. Mona's contorted form before him seemed to match the sound of the word. "You were so very beautiful that the only word for your exquisiteness was pulchritude. What a horrible-sounding word to describe such incredible beauty. It sounds like some terrible affliction. And now, my poor Mona, it seems to fit." Her twisted body hid her beauty from him as much as her madness had.

"I am so sorry. It would have been better if you had died." He expected no response from her, but his repentance churned in his stomach at these words.

Oliver made his way back to the subway in the half-dark of early evening. The days were becoming shorter and colder. Soon there would be snow. He'd have to purchase winter gear. A heavy, wind-proof coat, warm boots, gloves, scarf—the weightier items he had not needed in Vancouver. Listing these items kept his thoughts from returning to the hopelessness that was Mona. She would need none of these things. She would likely not live through the winter, given her depleted form.

In spite of the sadness that followed him home after visiting Mona, dinner with Derek, Theresa and Gavin was a happy affair. They talked long into the night. It was after midnight when Derek and Oliver walked to the coach house. Settled in bed with a book in hand, Oliver sighed with satisfaction. Life had taken him down a turbulent river, and he had fought the current every inch of the way. It was good to let go of that struggle. Tomorrow, Gwendolyn and Dillon were coming to visit their uncle, and Oliver would be surrounded by those he loved most in the world. He had his family. He had a home. He had a good friend in Shirley. He needed nothing more.

Shortly after three in the morning, Oliver's phone rang. It was the nursing home. Mona was not doing well. Perhaps he should come and spend some time with her in case she didn't make it through to dawn. He tossed the blankets back and dressed quickly. Derek got up as well.

"I'll drive you," he insisted. "I'm not going in, but I'll drive you."

Oliver took him up on his offer. He did not wake Gavin or call Gwendolyn. No need to disturb them. There was nothing they could do. If she survived, they could, if they chose, have their chance to say goodbye in the light of day.

One of the nursing staff met him at the door and ushered him into Mona's room then left. She was breathing roughly, shallow and quick. He sat by her bed and reached out to hold her hand, but both were clenched under her chin. It was now or never, he though as he looked at her contorted body. She had been so beautiful, so very beautiful on the outside, but inside she was as hellish as she now looked, more so, in fact. Every time he taught *The Picture of Dorian Gray*, he'd thought of Mona. How unconscious the rest of the world was to the nightmare within her as they'd admired her beauty. Few had glimpses of that incongruity. Now, others would recoil from her physical state as he had from the horror within. Poor, poor Mona. How rare the beautiful moments. How she had suffered. How she had made him suffer. But he'd finally chosen to let go of the battle and to float down life's river hoping for a peaceful estuary. If he could withstand the whirlpool that was his life, perhaps that would be his reward. But he had to achieve forgiveness for that kind of peace.

"I suppose this is the time to get everything out in the open. First things first. Mona, I forgive you," he began. Once started, the list of things to be forgiven was not as long as the anger and resentment he'd nursed over the years led him to expect. "It's easy for me to forgive you for what you did to me—your attacks, the betrayal. Your cruelty. If it had just been me, you would have long ago gone to Hewitt. Maybe I was the one who was selfish. The kids may have liked to spend some time with their biological father. I could have been a bigger man, stepped aside, or even encouraged them."

"It is much harder for me to forgive you for how you treated the children, but then again, that's between you and Gavin and Gwendolyn. I cannot forgive you on their behalf, but I can acknowledge the suffering you must have gone through had you any idea of how they felt about you, Gavin in particular." Oliver fought the urge to stop altogether. He swallowed the rising bitterness in his throat at the thought of the children cowering in fear of their own mother. That was theirs to forgive or not, as they decided.

"I forgive you for destroying so much—our home, our family, the garden, my love for you. Some stubborn part of me still loves you, so you didn't completely succeed there." Oliver gave a sad twisted smile.

"I forgive you for the lifetime of lies. Perhaps I contributed to that. I could have been more compassionate, more sympathetic to your needs and what you were going through. I tried, but not hard enough it seems."

Mona's breathing became less labored. She seemed to be resting more peacefully, but that may have been his imagination as well.

"Please forgive me for not trying harder to get the help you needed. So many obstacles blocked the way—your mother being one of them, but I'm not going to lay blame on anyone but myself. I failed in so many ways. I knew your fear of being left alone, yet I told you often that once the children left and our debts were paid, I would leave you. I deceived myself, told myself that those words were not a threat, that I was doing you a favor by giving you fair warning. That part was a lie, but it was the only leverage I had. You used the children, and I used your fear. Forgive me."

Oliver rubbed his face. He placed both hands on the bed preparing himself for the rest of his confession.

"Something I have to tell you. Something I've been carrying around with me since the day I left to catch the train. I need to ask your forgiveness, but I don't expect it. How could you forgive what I did, or did not do? I was too much of a coward to admit it to anyone, but I must tell you this before you go just in case forgiveness is possible."

"The day I left for Toronto—when I stood before you in the garage, you up on the stool with the rope around your neck, and me carrying my backpack telling you to do whatever you were going to do because I was done—I heard. When I turned my back on you to head into the house, I heard the stool scrape the floor. I knew what you had done, but I didn't look back. I heard, or at least I believe I heard, you kick the stool out from under yourself, and I walked away. Finished. Exhausted. Tired of rescuing you only to be slapped in the face again and again. What kind of man does that, just walks away, closes the front door, and goes down the sidewalk? I stopped to chat with Mrs. White, told her I was going to see the kids, as if nothing had happened. And just as I told the police, I did not see the postman."

Oliver lifted his head and looked out the window. Speaking more to himself than to Mona, he said, "I must have been a block away when he found you and rescued you. I was probably on the bus when the ambulance came."

He stopped and looked back at the crumpled form of Mona. "And all the while I was on the train making calls back, I believed you were dead. Hoped you were dead although I was afraid to believe I was finally free. I left the messages to avoid suspicion. The police questioned me, and I answered as if I knew nothing."

Oliver paused at this. It was time for complete truth, not excuses. "I answered to avoid my own deliberate negligence, my culpability." He did not shed a tear, feeling nothing but the surety of unavoidable responsibility.

"You had the last laugh, however. You lived. You lived long enough to give me one last kick in the teeth. My heart attack just about did me in, but that was nothing more than I deserved. Mona, I am sorry. I am sorrier than I can ever express. If I had helped you, you could have had a much better recovery. If I had helped you, you would still be part of my life. And that is why I left you there. I chose freedom. But I will never be free, not from my culpability. That I could do such a thing will haunt me forever. I've changed my name, but not who I am." Shirley's words to Gavin sounded clearly, and he added, "I will have to work to turn that around."

Empty of explanation and supplication, Oliver rested his head on the bed. Mona's breathing was definitely more relaxed. As he listened to her inhale and exhale, he fell asleep, but for how long, he was not sure. A hand on his shoulder woke him. The sun shone in the large window of the room. He sat up and looked at Gavin and over at Gwen. How long they had been there? Had they heard his confession? Did they know what he'd done? He'd never ask. He hoped never to speak of his actions again even if he had to carry the burden alone for the rest of his life.

"She's gone, Dad," Gavin said. He did not cry. Gwendolyn blotted her tears as they came.

Oliver looked at Mona. Finally, she was at rest. Finally, her ordeal was over.

Chapter 24

After the brief reprieve of mild weather, winter came in with a frigid blast. Every unsalted surface sent pedestrians sprawling and cars helplessly spinning. Oliver's new wool coat, heavy as it was, offered little warmth against the freezing temperatures and cutting wind.

Oliver unwound his scarf and shed his snow-covered coat in the doctor's waiting room. Other burdens would not be so easily removed. Before his grandchild's expected arrival, Oliver had to deal with the past and stop pretending it had not happened. He'd long beaten himself up with guilt and fear but was not clear about how to prevent it from bleeding into the present. With the therapist Dillon recommended, he shared the events leading up to his ultimate act of hatred. The man listened as Oliver struggled to explain how he'd time and time again rescued Mona from other suicide attempts, many of which were just for show, but some were real attempts. He told the therapist how he had tried to get her help and about the indifference of officials along the way.

"Nobody seemed to want to get involved. Nobody believed me. That was the worst of it. No one took my concerns seriously enough to step up and get her the help she needed," he said over and over again. Everyone had walked away in one form or another and left her, the children, and him, hanging, a point brought home, finally brought to heart, with the telling and retelling.

"Would rescuing Mona have made any difference? You were leaving her no matter what she did. Had you saved her that last time, would she have made another attempt?"

The answer was obvious. She certainly would have, but he knew he had a moral obligation to prevent anyone from harming themselves or others. Did he also have a legal responsibility? Would the police show up at his door after years of investigation, determining what must have happened?

"It sounds to me like there is plenty of blame to go around for Mona's state. You say you heard the stool being kicked out from under her. Are you sure you heard it?"

"No, I'm not one hundred percent sure, but obviously she was standing on it right in front of me with the rope around her neck. It was clear what she intended to do."

"Hadn't she done that before and not gone through with it?"

"Yes, but most often I stopped her, pulled the rope off and got her down. But not this time."

"I'm not trying to make excuses for you, Oliver. You just need to be sure about what happened. Had you ever walked away from her when she tried this before?"

Oliver listed the times he'd called her bluff. Yet he had stopped her from cutting her wrists although she could have just as easily turned the knife on him. He had shouted at her and ripped the plastic bag off her head when she'd threatened to suffocate herself. But he had walked out of the room once when she stood on the bed with a rope tied to the light fixture in the center of the ceiling. It would not hold, as she well knew. It was all for show.

"What she was about to do was obvious. I didn't even tell her to get down. I just turned my back and walked away."

"Why did you do that?"

"Because I was tired. Bone-weary of it all. Was peace, some normalcy, too much to ask for?"

"Was she tired, too? Tired of living with herself, her behavior?"

"I'm sure she was, but I am also sure that she was afraid of being left alone, and I was leaving. I gave her fair warning," but he stopped. It sounded too much like an excuse, and there was no excuse for either walking away or threatening to leave. "That had to have pushed her over the edge."

"You are telling me that if you had stayed, she never would have attempted suicide again."

He didn't answer. She would have kept it up until she was successful one way or another.

"And are you telling me that when you turned your back on her that last time that you knew she would go through with it, that she wasn't simply making an empty threat again?"

"No, but I heard the stool scrape the floor. I'm sure of it."

"Are you sure of it or are you simply adding up the details and coming up with what fits your sense of responsibility, your loyalty to someone who couldn't appreciate it, your feelings of guilt for deciding to free yourself from an untenable situation?"

"I heard the stool scrape the floor. I am not sure, but I think it happened."

"You say you turned your back, walked through the house, grabbed your suitcase and went out the front door. Did you lock the door?"

"No, I didn't. I shut the door and stood there for a minute. I walked by the window of the garage, but I purposefully didn't look in. I went down the sidewalk and talked to Mrs. White, my neighbor for a few minutes."

"About how long? Five minutes, ten?"

"Perhaps five. She asked after the kids. I told her I was leaving for good, that the house would be empty by the end of the month. We talked about her roses, the grass. I'd cut ours shorter than usual because I wouldn't get the chance to mow the lawn again until I came back to close up."

"What direction did the mail deliverer usually come? From Mrs. White's place to yours or from the other direction."

"Usually, he dropped her mail off first then ours."

"And you didn't see him coming up the street as you spoke to Mrs. White?"

"No," and with a note of surprise he added, "and I walked toward the way he would have come as I went to the bus stop."

"How far to the bus stop?"

"About ten minutes away."

"Add it up, Oliver. You walked away from Mona, went through the house, got your suitcase, walked out the door and paused for a moment. Then you spent about five minutes talking with Mrs. White and another ten minutes to the bus stop all the while not seeing the mail deliverer come up the street. It was at least fifteen minutes since you left Mona. The human brain can only survive for about ten minutes without oxygen. If anyone was able to save Mona, she must have hanged herself long after you left. Didn't you say the front door was open when the mailman came to the house, and that's why he thought something was wrong? Who opened the door after you left, Oliver?"

He had nothing to say. He did not have the answer. She could have been having an affair with the mailman, and that is why he walked into the house and then the garage only to discover her hanging, but no matter how it added up, the math didn't work to support Oliver's guilt.

"Even in my line of work, Oliver, I cannot save those who are determined to do harm to themselves. I have every tool in the toolbox to try to help, but there are no guarantees. Mona was determined to end her life. Maybe she was, as you were, bone weary of herself and her life as well. We all have the right to take risks. This may have been a risk Mona was willing to take."

Oliver heard the words, but they were not making the long trek from his head to his heart.

"Frankly, Oliver, your belief that somehow you were in charge of Mona or that it was even possible for you to overcome her state of mind is, well, arrogant. You are lucky. Your children are proof that good came out of that nightmare of a life, and you can take much credit for that."

Oliver wasn't offended by the doctor's blunt talk. He could focus on nothing beyond calculating the timing of his leaving and Mona's suicide. Without saying anything besides thanking the therapist, Oliver left the office when his session was over. He had to find out. He'd not asked for the police records for fear that they would put two and two together and discover his complicity. But he had to be sure. The only way he could be convinced was by speaking with the postman, but he didn't know who the man was. Perhaps Mrs. White did.

Her number was disconnected. He had to go to Vancouver. He had to get concrete details before he could relinquish his culpability at least for her last cognizant performance, if not for their tempestuous lives.

"At least you'll be getting a break from this wretched winter," Gavin said as he took Oliver's suitcase out of the trunk.

"That's why I'm going, that and to see Shirley and Mrs. White. I don't know what's happened to our old neighbor, but I'm going to find out where she's moved, if she's still with us. And the police asked me to pick up Mona's belongings. I've been putting it off." While all that was true, Oliver hadn't told anyone the real reason he needed to be in Vancouver. Gavin and Gwen would not have understood, or worse, would have found it horrifying. He would not confess to them what had transpired, coward that he was, and burden them with his complicity in their mother's attempted suicide. If he could get the facts, maybe then.

"Don't stay too long. The baby is due in a little over a month. You'll be here for that, won't you?"

Did Gavin need reassurance that Oliver wouldn't miss what was the most important event in his life next to the birth of his own two? He embraced Gavin and gave his back two big thumps. "I wouldn't miss the birth of my first grandchild for anything. Don't worry. I'll make it back if I have to hitchhike across the country." Oliver held him at arm's length and looked squarely into his eyes.

It was late afternoon when the plane landed in the gloom and rain at YVR. Oliver took the Skytrain downtown and trudged from the station to his hotel. He was overdressed and overheated in the heavy wool coat that reached below his knees. The frigid cold of Toronto had erased all memory of the mild and wet Vancouver winters. He'd spend the rest of the day looking for a raincoat and visiting familiar places on Robson Street. Tomorrow would be soon enough to go to the old neighborhood and find the postman or at least discover who he was. Tonight, he would be a tourist in his old home town.

Just in case the postman was early, Oliver arrived at nine in the morning at the home in which Mrs. White had lived. The new occupant appeared cautious. Half hidden behind the door, she said that Mrs. White moved into a senior's residence, Crofton Manor, in Kerrisdale, just a few miles away by bus. He asked when the mail was expected, explaining that he'd lived next door, and as an excuse, he said that he was awaiting some important documents recently mailed.

"Never before noon," the woman said and promptly closed the door.

Chapter 25

Oliver got a coffee to go from his favorite coffee shop on campus. While the campus itself appeared dreary in the misty rain, it was also familiar and comforting. He took in the scene of students rushing from and to exams—it was that time of year—or catching up on sleep in lounge chairs strewn throughout the lobby. He had to fight the urge to visit the bookstore to see what texts his colleagues had ordered for their courses. He did not go to the English department, fearing that catching up with colleagues would take too much time and he'd miss the postman. Perhaps he'd come back later. Perhaps not.

The familiar walk from campus to his old house filled him with nostalgia. He could just about adjust his memories to filter out the awful past. That is, he could until he reached his street. It was eleven thirty. He would wait on the corner until the postman came to avoid looking like a dangerous character skulking outside the door of Mrs. White's former home.

He could see the postman approaching, but the gait, the carriage of the body told him it was not a man but a woman. His disappointment hit him physically. He waited nevertheless.

When she came up to him, he spoke. "Hello, I would like to speak with you for a moment, if I may." He tried to sound harmless, non-threatening.

"Sure," she said, "how can I help you?"

Oliver explained who he was, the husband of the woman who hanged herself, and that he had to talk to the postman who found her and helped her. He wished to express his appreciation and to ask him a question for his own peace of mind.

"Ralph, he's a good friend of mine," she said. "He had to take some time off—stress leave—after that. It really shook him up." She put down her heavy mailbag, willing to give Oliver her time.

"I can imagine. It was good of him to help. Heroic. I need to talk to him. Just for a moment. I have only one question."

"Shoot," she said. "I know all about that day. We've gone over and over it, Ralph and I. I can probably answer your question and give him your thanks without upsetting him all over again."

She was warning him, Oliver understood. She was not going to let him distress her friend. "Can you tell me what time the postman, Ralph, found Mona? You see, I left that afternoon for the train to Toronto to see my—our—children. We were separating, divorcing, and I feel like hell that maybe I could have done something." How easy it was to speak with a complete stranger, now that there was a chance, no matter how minuscule, that he hadn't walked away from her as she was dying.

"Oh, sure. That's easy. One of the collection boxes on this route was broken into that day, and Ralph had to wait for our district supervisor and the police to come. That took a while, and he was already late because of a mix-up with the fliers. He got to your place, or your old place, a little after three that day. He called me to come and get him. He was too shaken up to drive. I finished my round at three-thirty, and he was still speaking with the police when I picked him up. We've traded routes. He couldn't take it, coming back here."

With a deep breath, eyes closed, Oliver let her words reverberate through him. Three o'clock. Not two. Not ten minutes after two. Three o'clock. He opened his eyes full of tears and smiled at her. "Thank you," he breathed. "Thank you. And please thank your friend for me. Give Ralph my most profound thanks."

"Will do." She picked up her bag and, walking away, said, "You have yourself a good day."

He found Mrs. White and chatted with her briefly then stopped in to see Shirley, who was her chipper self, if not as steady on her feet as she was the last time they'd met. She begged off going out for dinner, sighting her advanced years and arthritis acting up in the damp weather. Before returning to his hotel, Oliver stopped in at the police station to pick up Mona's belongings. There was very little—her rings, a watch, his letter and the envelope of money. It was a lot of money—enough to cover Mona's expenses for the month, and more to secure a new apartment in Vancouver. At the red light of a pedestrian crossing, Oliver thrust the envelope into the hand of a young father who had a stroller and was holding the hand of a toddler. He quickly walked away without saying a word. Time to fly home.

In the early spring after Sophia Gwendolyn's birth, Gwen and Oliver went to the Toronto cemetery where Mona's ashes were kept behind a plaque on a wall of such commemorations. Flowers in the small vase aside her name surprised them. A tiny bouquet of one each of red, white, pink, and coral-colored roses.

"Did you bring these?" he asked Gwen, but she hadn't, and he had not. It might have been Theresa, but both of them knew it wasn't.

"Perhaps he is coming to terms with her," Oliver said. Gwen put her arm through his and pulled him to her.

Oliver carried eighteen-month-old Sophie through the front door of the Rook Center for Survivors. "Say hello to Mrs. Brown, Sophie. Wave," Oliver said as he smiled at the child and then at the receptionist behind the large counter.

"They're waiting for you, Oliver. You have five customers today," Eleanor Brown said, "six, counting Miss Sophie."

Oliver strode into the large bright playroom where children ranging from one to four entertained themselves, their parents watching, waiting for him. Today, Gavin provided his pro bono legal services for families of those living with a child or spouse with mental illness. He gave one full day a week to the center. Gwendolyn was on staff full-time. She chose counseling these same families as her life's work. Dillon as well counseled one afternoon a week. Although they employed a child-care professional, she was off sick today, so Oliver offered to fill in for the afternoon session, relieving Theresa who'd agreed to cover the morning.

"How's he getting along?" Gavin asked Gwen.

"Just look at him," she said from the doorway of the playroom. "He's loving it."

And he was. Oliver sat on the floor as two one-year olds climbed onto his lap. He was leading the children in a song he used to sing to Gavin and Gwendolyn when they were young. Dipping each hand one at a time like a whale diving through the water, Oliver sang:

"An Orca whale with a great big tail,
Little white oysters and an Orca whale.
An Orca whale with a great big tail,
Little white oysters and an Orca whale."

He thumped his fists against his chest and sang out:

"Sea otters and seagulls."

Pinching his fingers together as he held his hands shoulder high, he continued his song:

*"Little white oysters and an Orca whale.
Sea otters and seagulls,
Little white oysters and an Orca whale."*

The children loved the song and imitated Oliver's actions as he sang it again. Gwendolyn and Gavin joined in for the second round.

The center opened just after Sophie's first birthday, but the plans for the center began shortly after Oliver's trip to Vancouver. He kept his appointments with the therapist, and as he progressed, the idea came to him. Both Gavin and Gwendolyn were on board immediately, as was Dillon. Shirley helped with the necessary accreditations and with connections for fundraising and grants, and they were open for business.

Once the center was on its feet, Shirley announced, "You're on your own now. I've done all I can. The rest is up to you. I'm not going to be making any more trips to Montreal. I'm getting too old for all this running around. My family and friends are going to have to visit me in Vancouver." That she meant what she said was clear, for Shirley didn't mince words.

"We'll miss you," Oliver said. "I'll miss you. But count on it. I'll be out to visit at least once a year, if not more." He meant this as well.

When he wasn't engaged in childcare, Oliver kept himself busy on the board of directors and with further appeals for grants. He also did the writeups for publicity.

That afternoon, Gwendolyn and Gavin stayed behind for a staff meeting at the center, and Theresa picked up Sophie. Oliver needed to do some shopping so would make his own way home. It was nearing the end of August, and although the summer had been suffocating with its heat and humidity, a touch of autumn brushed the early evening air. Oliver walked the tree-lined streets and noticed a tinge of red and gold on a few towering maples. While some mourned the passing of summer, Oliver welcomed the fall. He'd always felt that autumn was what all of nature worked toward—a fulfilment of purpose, harvest, the golden crown.

His life had taken a turn he'd never allowed himself to dream of and come to fruition in ways that surprised and humbled him. First, his granddaughter. Sophie was a beautiful child with her father's and grandmother's stunning blue eyes. She was a calm, delightful baby who laughed with ease. She loved her grandpa and he doted on her. Were the long years of misery worth it? How could he answer such a question? It had been his life, what he'd been given, what he'd chosen. He'd lived it with as much integrity as he had. Not perfectly. Not without fault. But he'd kept walking through hell and come out to this fair place.

/|\

"No!" cried Sophie.

"No? What do you mean, no? You've been asking for Grandpa all through dinner and bath time," Gavin said. He and Theresa had made a quick dash from their home to the coach house with Sophie who was in her pajamas and wrapped in a heavy blanket. Gwendolyn and Dillon had come earlier for dinner with Oliver.

"No!" cried Sophie again, pointing across Oliver's living room to the large windows. Christmas was nearing, the fireplace glowed as did the lights on the small Christmas tree.

"Snow!" five of them said at once. They stood before the window and watched large flakes dance their way to the chilled ground that accepted the blanket with grace. The gardens were prepared, tender plants long ago sheltered against killing frost, snug in their winter sleep. Oliver had made sure of that, had, after pruning, packed leaves around the rose bushes and covered non-resilient plants. All was safely sheltered. Not even the muffled promise of spring disturbed the calm.